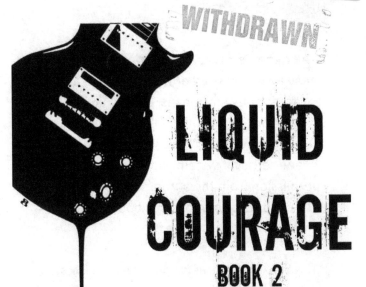

LIQUID

COURAGE

BOOK 2
IN THE LIQUID REGRET SERIES

BY MJ CARNAL

Cover Model: Lance Jones

Cover Photographer: Michael Meadows

Cover Designer: Cover Me, Darling

Editor: Kellie Montgomery

For Mom.

For being my hero and showing me what love truly means.

PROLOGUE

I can't sleep. I've been trying to reach Della for hours. It's not like her to ignore her phone. We've got two shows in Arizona and a quick stop in Vegas before we head back home. I can't wait to sleep in my own bed. I can't wait to hold her. I'm not complete unless she's with me. We've been together for as long as I can remember. We were kids when we met and neither of us ever looked back. I couldn't wait to marry her, to mark my territory. If it's true that you get one true love, I was lucky enough to find mine early. That just gives us more years to be together.

The walls of the hotel room are closing in on me. It's close to three AM and I can't find her. I've tried Laney and Mia a few times but no one's answering. I can't help the panic that's bubbling up. We've had so many threats, so many weird things happening. I've upgraded our security system. I've hired extra men to protect her. My manager, Joshua, assures me that we've got the best in the industry. Truth be told, I wish they'd pull the security detail off of me and put them all on Della.

I knew there'd be a price for fame. I've given up sleep, time with my friends and family, time away from home. I've slept on a cramped tour bus, some seedy hotels, some awesome suites and a bunk inside my trailer when I'm on tour. I wouldn't trade it for anything in the world. I just wish that Della would agree to come on the road with me.

Most of the threats have come to me. Some people are really sick. It's bad enough to deal with the women groping me when I walk by, but some of the things left in my dressing room really disturb me. Lately, I've been getting notes saying if I don't leave Della, I'll be sorry. When she got her first threat at work, I made her quit. She was pissed at me but I honestly didn't care. Her wellbeing is my number one priority. I couldn't live one day on this Earth without my wife.

I reach for my phone and try her number again. Straight to voicemail. I dial Lex and wait. He's the best security guard we have and I know he's on duty tonight. No answer.

"Shit!" I throw my phone across the room.

It's getting harder to breathe. I know something's wrong. I need to get my shit and pack up. Time to go. Joshua can kiss my ass. I just need to see her to know she's ok.

A soft knock on my door grabs my attention. I look through the peephole and see Damien. I take my first breath in about two hours. I asked him to find her and he's never let me down. I yank the door open and my eyes lock with his.

I think I'm going to throw up. His eyes are completely void and his face is pale. He's walking into my room like a zombie. Is he awake? Then I see them. Joshua, Max, Chance. They're all here and standing outside my room.

"Harley?" Damien's voice cracks and I know. He doesn't need to say anything else.

I shake my head. "No." Tears are filling my eyes and no one is saying anything. "No. No. No."

"Lex called. I'm sorry, man. I'm so fucking sorry." It's like I'm in a tunnel. Damien's words barely register.

My legs go out from under me. I feel my knees crash against the floor but there's no pain. I can't breathe. I'm gasping for air. She's gone. She's gone. It's like someone is reaching into my chest and yanking my heart out while it's still beating.

There's so much pain. I scream out, the noise not even recognizable. I want to wake up. Please, God, let me wake up. I don't want to be in this nightmare anymore. Please.

I feel Damien pull me against him. His body is trembling and I can feel his tears on my bare chest. He's whispering over and over again. "I'm so sorry. I'm so sorry."

"The plane leaves in about an hour. I've cancelled the next few stops." Joshua is on his knees next to me but I don't care. "We can make all the arrangements for you. Whatever you need, Griff."

I'm trying to gulp in some breaths. I can't breathe. My lungs are burning and I might pass out. Damien's grip tightens on me as the rest of the band starts packing all my stuff.

"It can't be true." I gasp. "I want to wake up, D. Please. Wake me up."

"I can't." His voice breaks.

I push to my feet and grab for Joe. He's been outside my door tonight to keep me safe. What a fucking joke. They've failed. My wife is gone. My feet are unsteady and as I start to fall, I grab for the weapon at his hip. He's faster and instead of letting me have it, he grabs me and lowers me to my knees.

"Please, Joe." I'm begging. "Please."

He pries my fingers from the butt of the gun. I have no strength left and I crumple onto his feet. His strong hands reach for me but stop when I wail. She's gone and I can't face another second without her.

"Kill me." My voice sounds so foreign. "Please, Joe. I can't live without her." When he doesn't move, I look into his eyes. He's holding back his tears and it breaks me even more. "Please. Kill me, too."

Joshua is at my side, needle in hand. Police surround us. My brothers are at my side. I hear myself begging to die. When the needle leaves my arm, I feel the warmth spreading throughout my veins. I can't keep my eyes open. Damien lowers me into his lap and watches as I fall under Valium's spell.

Chapter 1

"Fuck." I can't feel my legs. I grab for the kitchen counter but miss it completely, spilling my drink all over the floor. "Shhhhh."

Oksana's giggle fills the room. I can't really stand this bitch but her endless supply of drugs keep me warm at night. "Let me help you."

As she bends over, she loses her balance and pulls me down with her. Now we're both laughing so hard that I can't breathe. "We have to be quiet. Damien's going to be pissed if we wake them up."

"Fuck him." She crawls to the fridge and pulls out the bottle of wine that Mia put in there for girl's night tomorrow night. As she takes a long pull straight from the bottle, I can't help I don't care that it's not ours to drink. "Want some?"

I crawl toward her and open my mouth. She pours it down my throat and climbs into my lap. The sweetness of the liquid shocks me and I almost lose whatever food might be left in my stomach. I don't remember the last time I ate anything. Shit, I don't remember the last time I did anything other than numb myself with anything I can find. When she offers me another sip, I shake my head.

She grinds against my lap. My body couldn't perform right now even if I wanted it to. I don't feel anything anymore. I don't even let myself feel the pain anymore. Let her get off. I could give a shit. What interests me most is that I know she has a clear plastic baggie in her pocket that holds the key to a good night's sleep tonight.

I grab her hips, guiding her over my lap. In a minute, she'll be lost and I'll be able to pluck those perfect pills right from her pocket.

"Harley." She grabs my hair as her jeans rub against my shorts. "This feels good."

"Whatever you need." My fingers rub over the top seam of the plastic bag.

"I need this without the clothes." She grabs at my shirt and just like that, the pills are forgotten.

I pull her hands off of me. This can't happen. She's the only person in the world that understands why I need the pills, the liquor. She's the person I can call in the middle of the night when I need something that the bottle can't cure. She's a sure thing if I ever need it. But she isn't Della and I will not sink my cock into her body. Not tonight.

My head is spinning. I reach for the wine bottle and chug it. Oksana's voice is echoing through the kitchen but I don't have a clue what she's saying. I don't give a fuck either. The only thing on my mind is the fine line I'm teetering on. I'm one step closer to that beautiful moment when the world goes black. The moment when everything is silent and I have no awareness that I'm even still alive.

"Harley!" Oksana screams and stomps her feet. "You need to get over her. Let it go! Look at me."

I try to bring my eyes up to meet hers. My head is so heavy. "What?" My voice is slurred, foreign.

She grabs the wine bottle and smashes it against the counter. The remaining drops of happiness run down the kitchen island and glass covers my legs, the floor, it's everywhere. I just stare at the slivers that litter the floor. Several pieces are sticking into my skin but I can't feel them. It's a combination of grief, complete intoxication and the lack of any feelings left in my life. I have a fleeting image of slashing my wrist and letting go of all the struggles. All the bullshit. All the loneliness.

With shaking fingers, I reach for the jagged bottle. What would it feel like to leave all of this behind? Would there be pain? Would it be complete freedom? A glimpse of Damien, Max and Chance flashes in front of my eyes and I drop it onto the floor with a crash. I clench my eyes shut, praying for the darkness to take me. It will be one more day behind me. One more day that I survived without Della by my side.

"What the fuck?" Damien is standing in the doorway of his kitchen glaring at us. I can't imagine what a mess we've made. My mind can't comprehend anything except that he looks pissed. He pulls his cell phone from his pocket and calls Joshua. "Send a driver over here. Time for Oksana to go home."

"I'm not going anywhere." She slips on the spilled wine and lands on her ass. She curls into a ball on the floor and reaches for me. Her fingers brush my bare legs. I just stare at them. They're long and thin and perfect. Nothing like Della's were. Della was real. Every single part.

"Get her purse." Damien's words are quieter as he points at Mia.

"I'll carry her out.   Just leave the mess."

"I'll start cleaning up."

That voice catches my attention.   It's like being stuck in quicksand. I raise one arm and reach for her but Damien slaps my hand away.

"Laney, don't even come in here. You're barefoot. There's glass everywhere. Just leave it." Damien picks Oksana up like she weighs nothing. She protests but her eyes close and she's out.

I put my head back and rest it against the island. The edges of my world are starting to blur. I'm close to letting go for the night. I'll wake up tomorrow and do it all again. I never know where I'll wake up. Damien moves me every night once I'm gone.

Some mornings, I wake in a pool of my own vomit. Just another reminder of how glamorous my life has become. Another stab in the chest reminding me that Della's gone forever.

Now the problem is my brain. Worthless piece of shit. My heart and soul belonged to Della. But my brain has started to work again and with that, the realization that there's someone in this world that makes me stop. Not for long and not on purpose. But she exists in my space and I can't seem to shake the nagging intrusion of my worthless brain. I can smell her. Her gardenia shampoo has become a familiar smell. It calms me every time I smell it. I can hear her voice but her words are foreign. I groan as a larger piece of glass is pulled from my leg. The sting is welcomed. Her hands are soft and cold against my legs. My body responds instantly and I begin the mental battle of right vs wrong.

Della has been gone five months. Five long, torturous, agonizing months filled with darkness. I never went back to the house. Joshua packed up all our things and put everything in storage. I tried to heal. I tried everything I could. Every night I stared at the bottle of Jack that Mia bought when they first moved in to their new house. I tried to focus on what Della would have wanted for me. I stayed strong for as long as I could. One night, her voice wasn't as loud. It was like I was forgetting the sound of it and it was too much to take. I scrolled through Damien's phone and found Oksana's number. That night, she brought me some pills that took all the pain away. I was at peace for a few hours. It was the first time since the night Damien showed up in the hotel room and gave me the news.

My life ended the night hers did. When she took her last breath, she took mine with her. When she closed her eyes for the last time, I stopped seeing. When her heart beat for the last time, mine stopped too.

Chapter 2

    "Can you hear me?" I pick a few more pieces of glass out of Harley's leg. I'm not even sure he knows I'm here. Every time I yank a little too hard, he grunts. I'm so angry. I've watched this downward spiral for far too long. He doesn't deserve this. But the way he's choosing to deny instead of heal has me ready to scream.

    When Damien and Mia bought this place, Joshua suggested Harley stay with them for a while. I don't think anyone objected. Max and Chance grabbed some clothes from his place and got him settled. Looking back, I think the transition from Max's place to this one was a bad idea. Max is single, quiet, full of life. Here, he has to witness Mia and Damien in the honeymoon phase of their relationship. It has to be a constant reminder of everything he's missing.

Harley smiled in the weeks following Della's death. They were few and far between but we saw them. We all had high hopes. Rachel, the grief counselor the label hired, had spent hours every day helping him through the early days. They'd gone back out on the road and finished their tour. It gave him purpose. It gave him a schedule and responsibility.

When they came home, the drinking started. I blame that bitch, Oksana, for a majority of this fuck up. There's something about her that I can't stand. She walks around here like she's meant to be here. She's toxic and Harley is too weak to see it.

I don't stay here much. Mia and I try to spend every Saturday having girl's night in. At first, I stayed every weekend. But hearing Oksana getting off every night changed my mind pretty fast. I never hear a peep from Harley. Sometimes I wonder if he's even aware of what's happening. I can't imagine a world where Harley is fucking her. Not her. I know we all grieve differently and I won't judge him. I just pray I'm wrong.

We'd gotten pretty close in the month after Della left us. There were moments when I would catch him watching me and my heart would flutter. I'd probably imagined it but that didn't stop my heart from hoping that someday I'd get a chance to make him happy. We were all still in shock and turned to each other for strength. Max spent time with Rachel and was able to talk about his feelings for Della openly with all of us. I think that helped Harley heal. To know she was so loved made us all realize how blessed we'd been. It was easy to be around Harley. He was always writing music and playing it for me. His world had been turned upside down but he was able to stay afloat. I miss him. I miss our friendship.

"You smell good." His voice startles me. His eyes are open and glassy. They flutter closed again.

I put my hands on his cheeks and make him look at me. "I refuse to watch you fade away. It was a tragedy, but you're still here. Don't you dare leave me." I brush his hair off his forehead and he leans into my touch. "Do you hear me, Griffin Miles? You need help. I can't watch this."

"Lane." His voice is barely a whisper as his body goes limp right in front of me.

I sit across from him and pull my knees into my chest. My eyes fill with tears. The strong, larger than life man who I used to fantasize about is a broken shell of the person he used to be. I can feel my heart rip in two. His love for Della was legendary. *IS* legendary. Watching them together used to give me hope that someday I'd find a person that I could love like that. Seeing him now makes me never want to find it. If finding it means losing it like this, count me out. I wouldn't survive it. I wouldn't have made it through the first night.

Della's death is still unsolved. Her autopsy report is due to be released to Harley this week. Because it's an active murder investigation, he hasn't been able to get many answers. I just pray that the report, no matter how gruesome, gives him a little closure. I've prayed every night that we'll find out that the first or second stab was the fatal one and that she didn't suffer. It would answer so many questions. Why didn't Lex hear anything? Why didn't she scream? Maybe she couldn't. Maybe it was fast and she didn't know it was happening.

"Is he out?" Damien's voice makes me jump. He puts his hand on my shoulder. "Sorry."

"It's ok. I was just thinking about Della." I look into his bright, blue eyes. "Do you think the autopsy is going to give him any peace?"

Damien sighs and looks out the back windows. He has that far off look that he gets every time he struggles to keep his emotions in check. "I can't imagine how it could. It would be horrible to lose Mia. I don't know if I could read about all the details."

"Damien," I whisper. "We have to do something. We can't keep this up. He's killing himself. I don't know how you can watch this happening, it's killing me. This has to be so hard for you guys."

Damien's voice breaks and he clears his throat. "I lost Della. I'm afraid if we send him away, I'll lose him too."

I shake my head. I can't even pretend to know what he's feeling. "Let's get him to bed. He can't stay like this."

Damien helps me to my feet and we work together to move Harley somewhere more comfortable. "You want him in your room tonight, Lane?"

I look at Harley. He's so at peace when he's asleep. "Please. I want to be there in case he gets sick."

Movement wakes me from sleep. Harley is sitting on the side of the bed, feet on the floor, head in his hands. I take a second to appreciate his back before I speak. His skin is perfect, smooth, muscled. His posture shows complete defeat. I'm not sure if it's his head that's pounding or just the reminder that life goes on.

I reach out and touch him. He doesn't pull away but he's far from relaxed. "Can I get you something?"

He sighs. "My life back."

My heart breaks for him. "I wish I could." My voice is barely a whisper. When he doesn't respond, I'm not sure he's even heard me. But I would. I would give him every second back that he's lost. I would bring Della back. I would do anything to stop the slow death he's going through. This is the most honest and raw I've seen him in months.

"Why am I here, Lane?" He turns to look at me, his eyes bloodshot and searching. "Why did I wake up with you? There are four other bedrooms. Why am I in this one?"

"I was worried." Is it really that simple?

"I don't deserve that." He scrubs his hands down his face.

I can't watch this. I drag myself out from under the covers and kneel in front of him. "Listen to me and listen good. I'm going to say this once. Life fucking sucks. I get that. I can't even pretend to understand what's happening with you. People die every day. The rest of the world keeps going. Is that fair? Hell no. Is this the cruelest hand you could have been dealt? Yes. But Della would roll over in her grave if she knew what you were doing to yourself."

He puts his hand out to silence me. His eyes hood in anger and his teeth clank against his lip ring. "Shut the fuck up, Lane. I don't want to hear this bullshit."

I stand up and push him back onto the bed. I straddle him and pin his arms to his sides. He could easily push me off but his strength to fight no longer exists. "Too bad. You're going to listen. Drowning your sorrows doesn't bring her back. Those pills you get from Oksana? They make you weak. This pity party makes you weak. This desire to kill yourself, drink by drink, makes you weak. You used to be the strongest man I knew. You used to stand in stadiums that sat eighty thousand and you wouldn't even break a sweat. You used to pull Damien up when he'd fuck up on tour. You'd bust Chance's ass for being irresponsible. Whatever this mystery bullshit is with Max, you'd hide him, save him, protect him. Whatever. That was you, Harley. That was the man Della loved. This weak man? This is the one that spends every night with Oksana competing to see who can be the most fucked up. It's time for you to be honest with yourself and start feeling whatever this is so you can get the fuck over it."

I gasp for breath. I'm so angry. He doesn't even fight me. He doesn't even scream back. He just lies there looking through me. I refuse to believe we've lost him. I will fight for him until the day he dies. Which at the rate he's going, won't be long.

"Fuck you!" I scream and roll off of him. I've tried kindness. I've tried love. Now I'm just livid.

His laugh makes my jaw drop. I want to rejoice in the sound of it but I'm so mad that I can't think straight.

"It's fucking funny?" I yell. "You're killing yourself and you're fucking laughing?"

He rolls onto me and pins my arms above my head. He's taken control back and he's fuming. "You don't know anything about me,

Adelaine. You think you know how I'm feeling? How's this for honesty?"

He grinds his hips into me and I can feel his arousal. I gasp as he continues to rub against me. "Stop it." I punch his chest over and over.

He brings his face an inch from mine. "You want the truth? My wife was killed. The only person in the world I've ever loved was taken from me in the most brutal way possible. The only person who understood me. The only person who ever turned me on. The only one my body has ever enjoyed. The last couple months have felt like a lifetime. It's fucking torture."

He stands up and pulls me with him. He glares down at me, anger and something else crossing his face. His eyes search mine but I'm not sure what he's looking for. I want to push him away but he's reacting for the first time in months. I'm afraid to push him back into the black hole he's been living in.

"Oksana's safe. I couldn't fuck her even if I wanted to. She doesn't do this to me." He pulls my hand into his erection and pins it there. "I was never unfaithful to Della. I never saw anyone else. My wife is dead, Laney, and I can see you. That makes me a fucking asshole. I couldn't control what happened to her, I can't control my need for anything that will make me forget, and I sure as fuck can't control my guilt that I get turned on when I see you. So, forgive me if I don't stay sober long enough to make myself feel any worse."

He pushes me off him and heads for the door. I just sit here completely stunned. I know I should go after him. I know I should tell him that what he's feeling has to be normal. I know that he's heading straight for his next drink. I need a minute to regain a little composure. What the hell just happened?

Chapter 3

'More than five months have passed since we learned of the death of Della Miles, wife of lead guitarist Griffin Harley Miles of Liquid Regret. Police have not released any details of the murder and there have been no arrests. Sources close to the band tell us that the autopsy report will be released to the public later this week.'

I throw the remote across the living room. I'm furious and I'm ready to rip someone's head off. "Seymour!" My yell even scares me.

Josh comes into the living room, ear glued to his phone and a face void of any emotion. When he sees my face, he hangs up. "What?"

His defensive tone sends me further into my fit of rage. "What the fuck was that?" I'm pointing at the television like a lunatic. "Who the fuck is this source? You better pray to God it isn't you or you'll never see a dime of our money again."

"I don't have any idea what you're talking about." He stares at the TV that is now off. "Care to calm down and clue me in?"

"This is bullshit!" I roar. "Her autopsy is going to be leaked to those vultures and the investigation will be over. Some sick fuck will get away with killing her because the police can't do their job."

"Sit." It isn't a request, it's a demand. I'm too weak to even fight anymore. My breaths are coming in short bursts and my attitude hasn't even ruffled Joshua's feathers. "Once the autopsy is public, we can't stop anything. I know you're frustrated. I promised you'd see it before it was released and I keep my promises. I'm just not sure you're ready."

I rocket off the couch like someone's set me on fire. I shove him against the wall and put my face inches from his. "Don't fucking tell me what I'm not ready for. I'm living this nightmare all alone. You don't get an opinion. I want that report today. Make it happen."

I shove him away from the wall. As he stumbles to catch his balance, I have a moment of clarity. What if what I learn makes it worse? What if the broken heart isn't the worst part? What if it's the second part that kills me?

I slam the back door and storm into the yard. My hands are shaking.

I need a drink, a pill, anything. I shoot a text message off to Oksana. She'll be my salvation yet another night. Fuck what Laney said. She doesn't know what this feels like. She doesn't know the real me. If she did, she'd run. My mind is toxic, my poison hurts everyone around me. It's tarnished the band. It killed my wife.

"Fuck!" I scream and let my knees hit the grass. The wind picks up. It used to be a source of comfort, a glimpse at Della from the other side. Now it just taunts me. "Leave me alone!"

"Griff?" Max's voice is like nails on a chalkboard. I just want a few minutes of peace.

"Go away." I stare at the blades of grass. The wind stirs them and they sway slightly. It's bullshit that everything in life goes on. The sun comes out every day and the moon is a sure thing. The days are hard, but the nights, oh God. The nights are torture.

When the wind whips through the yard again, I hear Max sigh. He turns his head toward the sunshine and his arms open at his sides. His smile is genuine. "Hey, Dell," he whispers.

"You son of a bitch. She was mine. Not yours. You don't have the right to talk to her." I charge him and he loses his balance. He hits the ground hard and doesn't fight back. My fists make contact with his jaw, his chest, anything I can reach.

"Stop!" I can hear them running at me, yelling for me to stop. I can't. Max loved her. The betrayal is overwhelming. My fists continue to fly and Max covers his face. He's trying to get away. I can't stop myself. Everything is in slow motion.

Chance crashes into me, tackling me and pinning me to the ground. His eyes are full of fear and for the first time, I realize I'm out of control. My eyes search everyone's face. They're all scared of me. I back out of Chance's grip and sit up.

Max is lying on the ground, his body curled into the fetal position. Laney and Mia are on their knees next to him. His breathing is shallow and he moans into the dirt. My hand covers my mouth. What the fuck have I done?

"Don't try to move." Laney runs her fingers through his hair. Her eyes meet mine and pity flashes through them. She shakes her head before returning her attention to Max.

I'm not so lucky with Mia. She's on her feet stalking toward me. I'll take whatever she throws at me. I deserve it. I'm scrum and I know it. Her fiery anger is aimed at me and it's a bulls-eye.

"What the fuck is wrong with you? You could've killed him. What were you thinking?" Mia shoves me. I give her credit. She's poking the angry bear with a stick and that takes guts. "It's Max, you idiot. You need help. This is completely out of control."

Everyone holds their breath to see how I'll react. But, she's right and I know it. I *am* out of control. I have been since the second Damien walked into my hotel room and told me Della was gone. I don't know how to stop the anger. I don't know how to let go and start healing. I sure as shit don't know how to quit drinking.

When Oksana opens the back door, all heads turn toward her. She looks at us in confusion before an evil grin breaks out on her face. "Who'd you piss off, Max?"

"No. Not today." Damien is pushing her back into the house. "You're not welcome here anymore. You need to go."

Hell no. She's my distraction, my partner in crime. She's my amnesia. "If she goes, I'm going with her."

"Over my dead body." Joshua holds me back but I keep fighting to get to Oksana. If she goes, I go. It's simple. "Lex, remove Oksana before this gets any more out of hand."

A growl escapes my throat when I see Lex. He was on duty when Della was murdered. I've been over this in my mind time and time again. I shouldn't blame him. He was just as distraught at the rest of us. He'd been guarding Della for so long, he was like family. But, that was then. Now he's just the screw up that got my wife killed. He was reassigned to Oksana as soon as we returned from the tour. Joshua was worried that she'd be a target since we were spending so much time together. All I knew was that I didn't want him near me. Something didn't sit right with me and I was done ignoring it.

Max sits up and spits a mouthful of blood onto the grass. Laney helps him to his feet and my heart jumps in jealousy. I'm losing my grip on reality. Five months. That's not enough time to heal, it's not enough time to learn how to live again and it certainly isn't an acceptable amount of time to start responding to another person. I will never get serious again. I make this vow right now, right here, there will never be anyone in my heart again. I'll never lose like this again.

Max clears his throat and looks at me. His eyes are already swelling. I feel sick. I did this. "I was just coming out to let you know that Officer Reeves is here. He says Joshua called and asked for the autopsy early. He's in the library."

My feet can't move fast enough. Pushing past Oksana, I've completely forgotten my desire for artificial amnesia. She'll be here whenever I'm ready. For now, I need to know what happened to Della.

My hands are shaking. No one should ever have to go through this.

Maybe this was a bad idea. There's no maybe about it. This is the worst idea I've ever had. Reliving Della's final moments is a nightmare I won't ever wake up from. Tears stream down my face and the words become blurry. She suffered and it's the news I was praying I'd never get. Final stab wound count is thirty two. Cause of death, asphyxiation. Defensive wounds on the hands and forearms. Best estimate is fifteen minutes from first impact to time of death.

"Stab wounds consistent with two different weapons." I try to catch my breath.

Damien's eyes snap up to Officer Reeves. "He used two knives?"

Reeves sits down and takes a deep breath. "Stab wounds are consistent with two suspects. One much larger than Della, one nearly the same size."

I shake my head. "No. That can't be right."

"The wounds show two distinct patterns. Some are angled downward, indicating the suspect was above her chest. Based on Della's height, we estimate suspect number one is about six foot three. The second pattern shows stab wounds entering her body completely horizontal. This is consistent with a suspect that is similar in height." He opens the report to the diagram of Della's body. I gag as he puts his hand on my arm. "I know this is difficult. But the more you know, the more you may be able to help."

I push the report away from me. I can't see anymore. I'll never know what it's like to have a night of sleep without nightmares. I'll never forgive myself for not protecting her. I'll never get over this loss and I'll never be able to breathe without her. I'll walk through the rest of my days waiting to be judged for being incompetent, for not being a good enough husband to know the second she needed me. I will never forgive myself. I will never forgive myself. I can never forgive myself.

"Let's go." I grab Oksana's hand and pull her out the front door.

"Where are we going?" She runs to keep up with me.

"Your place."

Chapter 4

Laney

"Hey, Slick." I throw my gym bag onto the loveseat. "Your face looks so much better."

Max chuckles. The bruising that was deep purple is now a green hue. "Like the green, huh?"

I sit next to him on the couch. I'm sweaty and I'm sure I smell but I've made myself at home at Mia and Damien's house for the last week. Having my apartment painted was taking longer than I expected but being here isn't a hardship. I get to swim, use the gym, watch the waves. It's like a mini vacation from my real life. "I bet it's nice to be able to see out of the right eye again."

"It doesn't suck." He smirks. "Think of anyone you can hook me up with yet? I'm waiting for you to give in and just date me yourself."

"Shut up. You know that's not true." I smile when he winks at me. I wish I knew someone single that was good enough for him. "Besides, I needed to make sure you were going to survive the backyard attack before I got anyone's hopes up."

"It was touch and go there for a while." Max laughs when I smack him on the arm. "I'm not sure I'm ready to give up my nurse, though. I may need one more sponge bath."

I flutter my eyelashes at him. "Why, Mr. Callum, are you getting fresh with me?"

"Is it working?" He raises one eyebrow. Max is the sweetest man

I've ever met. I want him to find someone who makes him happy. He deserves so much.

"It might be." I giggle when he attacks my sides, tickling me into a state of hysteria. "Stop. I hate being tickled." I gasp for air and fight him.

"Torture at its finest." Max is chuckling as I kick and scream under him.

The front door slams and we jump apart. Harley stands in the doorframe, larger than life, glaring at us. "Am I interrupting?"

I scramble to my feet. He's been gone for a week and I've been out of my mind with worry. I practically throw myself at him, stopping just inches from him. My hands cup his cheeks and I search his eyes. "Are you ok?"

He doesn't say anything, just nods his head. It's been an emotional week. News of the autopsy hit the airwaves like wildfire. Speculation started immediately. I heard all the rumors. Everything from Harley having a lover and killing his wife to get her out of the way to a mob hit. I don't blame him for going underground.

"I've been so worried." I pull him against my chest and his breath hits me. No hint of alcohol, no hint of anything but mint. I tighten my grip around his neck. "Thank God you're ok."

His body sags against mine and he sobs. I hear Max get up and leave the room but I don't care. Harley's broken soul is begging for help.

"I fucked up." He gasps. His hands tangle in my hair and his eyes plead for forgiveness. "I can still taste her on my lips."

My heart rips in two. My bubble of denial pops and I freefall into reality. He's been with Oksana. The truth is like a punch in the gut. I don't trust my voice so I let my body language try to soothe him. I run my fingers over his face and plaster on the best smile I can. My eyes fill with tears. I can't help myself.

"I stopped it. I couldn't do it." Harley takes a deep breath. "I can still taste her lips. I feel sick."

I rub my thumb over his lips, desperately trying to erase her. When that's not good enough, I don't even think. I'm moving before I know what I'm doing. I pull him to me, sealing my lips over his. He freezes and the enormity of what I've done hits me. I jump back like I've been shocked. My hand flies to my mouth and my eyes widen in fear.

"Harley, I'm so..."

I'm cut off when his lips crash against mine. The kiss is hungry and predatory. He pulls my hair, angling my head back for a deeper connection. His tongue doesn't beg for entrance, he takes it. There's nothing gentle about this kiss. It's passionate, it's powerful, and it's almost desperate.

I pull his hair and he groans. He pushes me back against the foyer wall and presses against me. I can feel every beat of my heart. I feel every sound he's making as my body tightens in anticipation. It wouldn't take much for this to escalate into something we can't come back from.

When he pulls away from me, he doesn't go far. His forehead rests on mine as we both try to catch our breath. "Laney."

It's all he needs to say. I know it's too soon. I know he's not ready. I know I wouldn't forgive myself if I pushed him and I'll never be someone's rebound. I'm too strong for that and he's too important to me to let this ruin our friendship. He has a long road ahead of him. His drinking is out of control, his emotions are destroyed and his new found obsession with Oksana is completely unhealthy. I need to keep my distance for now.

"We can't do this." His voice is quiet. "I can't do this to Della. I know that might not make sense to you, but.."

"Shh. I get it. I do." I run my hands up and down his arms. "I'm just happy you're home. Please don't leave like that again."

"Sorry." Max's cheeks redden, knowing he interrupted something. "Joshua is here and he wants to set up a press conference about the autopsy reports. You don't have to do it but we want you to be there when we plan it."

Harley's eyes water. "I'm so sorry, brother. I snapped."

Max just smiles. "Water under the bridge, man." He squeezes Harley's shoulder and turns to walk away. "Meet us by the pool whenever you're ready. Take your time."

"What do you think they're talking about out there?"

"Why are you here?" I glare at Oksana as she picks at the salad I made for myself for dinner. "By all means, help yourself."

"Thank you." She's an asshole. There aren't any other words to describe her. I can't stand the sight of her. I hated her when she was interrupting things between Damien and Mia. Now, she's the toxic person that allows Harley to throw himself further and further down the black hole of drugs and alcohol. I can't help but wonder if he'd be so far gone if she weren't in the picture.

"Let me ask you again. Why are you here?" I put my hands on my hips. How does this bitch not know she isn't welcome here?

"Harley called me. He said he needed me." She just shrugs. If I punched her, would anyone stop me?

"He said he needed you? Or needed something you had?"

"Same thing. What's your problem anyway? Sore loser? Mad he picked me over you? You had to know you didn't stand a chance. Look at you. Tattoos, piercings, two toned hair. The trailer park called. They want their leader back."

No she did not. I take a deep breath and try to concentrate on not making things worse for everyone. The only explanation for her is that she has fried most of her brain cells. "As witty as that may be, I'm going to give you a ten second head start before I kick your ass."

"Harley wouldn't let you hurt me. I mean too much to him." She just continues to eat my dinner like she's been invited and this is the most welcoming place on Earth.

Damien slides the back door open and they all file in. Sensing the tension in the room, Max comes to stand next to me. As they surround me, I can't help but smile. She's honestly shocked that no one is showing her any loyalty. My inner child screams '*I told you so*'. In my mind, I'm sticking out my tongue and yelling neener neener.

"Harley?" She whines and bats her eyelashes at him.

When he doesn't answer, I have to let my immaturity out to play. I pull him to me and lick his neck. She glares at me.

"Mine." I laugh as Mia pulls me out of the room. I shouldn't be proud of myself. I shouldn't be giggling so hard. I shouldn't be listening to Mia laughing back. I can't help myself. That felt good.

Chapter 5

I hate sitting in the hot seat during press conferences. The lights, the cameras. As far as I'm concerned, all these reporters can kiss my ass. They've done everything in their power to ruin me. They've dragged Della's name through the mud and she was a fucking saint. They've suggested that I was having an affair and to prevent a pricey divorce, I hired someone to kill her. I heard that she took her own life. I even heard that Max was so jealous that he couldn't have her that he killed her so no one else could either. The stories make my stomach churn.

Yet, here I sit, opening myself up to further abuse because there's no privacy in the public eye. I chose this for myself and believe me, I've considered giving it all up. Della will come back and haunt me if I give up now. I pray for closure. I keep thinking the more the media knows, the more likely someone will admit to seeing something.

When Damien takes his seat next to me, the flashbulbs go off. I don't know how he deals with this shit every single day. Poor Mia. This has to be torture. I get my share of screams and panty throwing but I can still go into a McDonald's without being swarmed.

A sense of peace comes over me when I notice Dell's friends here. The girlfriends she called her best friends line the front row. Her boss and some coworkers are seated in the next few rows. I am honored by the love everyone had for Della. She was someone that could have changed the world. She already had. She'd changed mine.

"Ladies and gentlemen, thank you so much for coming today. We are going to give you an update on the investigation into Della's death and some information on upcoming future tour dates for Liquid Regret. I will open the floor for questions following the press conference. However, we ask that you respect how difficult this is for Harley and the other men in the band. If I feel that things are getting too personal or painful, I will pull the plug on questions and lead my men back stage. My main priority is their well-being and safety."

Joshua is a natural in front of the camera. In another life, he must have been an actor or a rock star. Cameras and crowds only feed his ego. And believe me when I tell you, his ego is pretty big. I have to give him credit. He gives up his entire life for us. We're his biggest clients and he represents us like we're the only ones. He takes a bunk on the tour bus, he sits in rehearsals and while we're all partying after a show, he's left to clean up the shit storm we leave in every city. He has no personal life, he has no time with parents or siblings, and I have never seen him with a woman. Maybe that's why he's so serious all the time. Shit, I should really be listening but I can't keep my mind from wandering.

"The band is scheduled for six more cities before they start laying down music for their next album. The songs that they have written have exceeded any of my expectations. The next album is going to be genius. Look for that early spring. We hit the first of the six cities in two weeks. We have upped security for the men and their families. We are taking the threat very seriously. Lex, our head of security, will be on the road with us. There are several other bodyguards, police officers and undercover officers that are making sure the rest of this family is secure."

There's commotion in one of the back rows and I can't help but stare. I know I should be paying attention to Joshua. I need to look like my heart is still in the band. But, it isn't. And it's hard to fake something when you're broken. Several of Della's coworkers are on their feet and there is a buzz in the room. Joshua stops the press conference as the officers attempt to quiet the crowd. The receptionist who always greeted me with a hug and smile when I would visit Dell at work is talking hysterically and waving her arms in the air. She's panicked and I want to go to her and find out what's happening. These people will always have a place in my heart. Dell was happy there and that means everything to me.

Movement behind me catches my eye. Lex has taken a few steps back, inching his way to the door behind us. I ask him what's wrong but he doesn't even make eye contact with me. A sense of dread comes over me as I look back to the crowd. Damien is on his feet and is standing at my side. His hand on my shoulder calms me but I have a feeling that my world is about to change forever.

The officer at the front of the room is pulling his cuffs from his pocket. I'm frozen in place. What the hell is happening? Police are leading people from the room. The back door is immediately blocked and Joshua is pulling me away from the stage. Guns are drawn and trained on Lex.

"What the hell's happening?" I'm being shoved behind another of our bodyguards. It's happening in slow motion.

I see Oksana standing just a few feet away. She's scared and my heart beats out of my chest. For as much as I don't like her sometimes, she's been a saving grace for me throughout this whole nightmare. I grab for her, my hand making contact with her fingers. Her eyes are wide and tears are streaming down her cheeks.

"Oksana!" I yell for her over the commotion.   She doesn't move toward me.

"No." The force of Joshua's voice snaps me back to the present.

Lex is standing on the stage staring me down. His eyes are full of hatred and his sneer makes me stand up a little straighter. He's being cuffed and the look on his face turns my blood to ice water.

"I'm not going down alone." Lex yells to me. "You've been sleeping with your wife's killer. Stupid fuck. You deserve every ounce of pain this causes you."

I look at Damien. Shock is written all over his face. He turns to Oksana and before I know it, he charges her. His words are almost incoherent as he holds her to the ground, his hands around her neck.

I can't comprehend what's happening around me. Joshua has me pulled into his side, my body guard shielding both of us from the reality of what's happening. Police are dragging Lex out in handcuffs and he spits at me when they pass. Damien is being cuffed for attacking Oksana, who is crying and begging them to let her go. She's pleading with them and denying any part in Della's death.

"Stop!" I scream and a few people still. I push past Joshua and stop right in front of Oksana. "O, please tell me this isn't true."

Her eyes meet mine and I have my answer. She doesn't have to say anything. Her guilt is written all over her face. When she opens her mouth to deny it, I just shake my head.

"Why?" My voice cracks with emotion as tears flow freely down my cheeks. "Why, Oksana? She was everything to me."

"She wasn't good enough for you." Her words are filled with venom. "You said I couldn't have you because of her. We needed to be together. It's the way it's supposed to be."

"Oh my God." My voice is barely a whisper. I want to tear her apart. I want to give Lex a taste of what Della must have gone through. But as my legs give out, I hit my knees with no fight left in me.

The man who spent years protecting someone who loved him like family, took away what mattered most to me in life. The man who sat at the table with my family during holiday meals betrayed me. The person I trusted my life with took away the very thing that made my life worth living.

Oksana stood by my side from the second Della was gone. She gave me comfort, she gave me strength, and she gave me the things that made me forgot for a few hours. She was a friend in the midst of tragedy. She was a shoulder to cry on.

I am completely numb as Joshua pulls me to my feet. I can't hear anything he's saying. I can't feel anything. I'm being led out the back door where cameras go off and microphones are shoved into my face. The other guys from the band are trying to push me through the crowd. I can't breathe.

Max grabs my arm and shoves me into the front seat of my car. I watch him in slow motion as he gets behind the wheel and starts the car. He's silent as we burn rubber getting out of the parking lot. My cell phone is ringing in my hand. I can't answer it. I need a drink. I need to numb. I need to disappear.

"I need a drink. Please, Max. I need you to drop me off." Is that my voice?

"Anything you need, brother." Max is speeding and I know he shouldn't be driving either. His heart was torn in two when Dell was killed and he and Lex had always had a close bond. "I can't believe this. Part of me refuses to believe it. This can't be real."

My mind flashes back to every part of my life that Lex was involved in. He was there for everything. He loved Della. He had to. How could he do this? And Oksana? I've dedicated so much time to trying to help her, to be there for her, to support her when times got hard.

In this moment, when I should be so angry that I can't see straight, all I feel is betrayal. I gulp for air. The last thing Della saw was two people she thought of as family taking her life away. She would have let them in the house without hesitation. She would have felt safe just having them near. She would have been completely blindsided. I have to believe that the shock of what was happening had to numb her pain. I have to convince myself that she left this world knowing that the other people in her life loved her completely. I hold onto the hope that she knew she was going to a better place and that she will spend the rest of the time I'm alive watching over me and making sure I make the right choices.

My hands shake and I fight the urge to give in to the bottle. I stare out the window and bite the inside of my cheek so hard that it bleeds. "Drive faster, Max."

He nods at me and takes the next corner at full speed. I know I'm only minutes away from what I really need to make it through the night.

Chapter 6

Laney

The thunder startles me awake. It's been a horrible sleep. Mia called me a few hours ago to tell me about the press conference. A bolt of fear passed through me knowing we had all been so close to Oksana and Lex. They'd been in the same room, sleeping in the same house. It seemed fitting that after the phone call, a storm came out of nowhere. We don't get many thunderstorms and when we do, I usually snuggle under a blanket and enjoy the sights and sounds. Tonight I feel lonely. I imagine it's Della and she's pissed that Lex and Oksana carried out the ultimate betrayal. If I was with her, I would shoot a bolt of lightning straight into Oksana's ass. The next bolt would shoot through Lex's balls and, just like that, a little justice.

I roll over and try to get comfortable. I stare at the alarm clock. Three AM. My alarm is going to scare the shit out of me in just a few hours. I groan.

A pounding at the door about stops my heart. My apartment is in complete darkness. I'm suddenly scared. The pounding starts again.

"Come on, Lane. The bad guys are behind bars tonight." I can't even convince myself. "Where are my big girl panties when I need them?"

I trip over about a thousand things on the way to the door. Suddenly my furniture has a vendetta against me. Standing at the door, I take a deep breath and tighten the sash on my robe. Show no fear. I rip the door open like I'm angry and my jaw drops.

"Harley?" He's soaked with rain. Water drips from his dark lashes and his shirt clings to every muscle. I'd like to be that shirt. He's shivering and I reach for him.

"I've been walking around for the last hour." Even though I've moved aside to invite him in, he doesn't make a move. "I wanted a drink."

"And you didn't have one?" My heart pounds.

He shakes his head. His eyes captivate me. I can't look away. "I need you, Laney."

I take his hand and pull him into the foyer. I'm suddenly nervous. I don't get nervous. "Anything, Griff. Whatever you need."

"Make me forget." He pulls me to him and buries his face in my neck. His whole body shakes as his arms wrap around me. "Just for a while, make me forget."

I'm not sure what he's asking me but I'd do anything for him. I let him hug me for as long as he needs. Feeling him pressed against me stirs feelings in me that I haven't felt in so long. "What can I do, Harley?"

He yanks the sash on my robe and pulls it from my shoulders. He tugs my hair and I feel it in my core. His breathing changes as he licks and bites my neck. His hand dips under my tank and flattens on my stomach. I can feel his fingers brush the edge of my breast. I can't help but moan softly.

Taking his cues from me, he rubs his hand over my bare breast, tugging my nipple gently between his fingers. My head falls back. It's been a long time. I may talk a big game, but it's been nearly a year since I've had any sexual contact and it's long overdue. My heart is screaming that I'm a rebound, a distraction. My body doesn't seem to care.

"Feel good?" Harley puts his forehead against mine and his chocolate eyes stare through me. I whimper when he tugs my nipple again. "I'm selfish, Lane. I can't give you anything but tonight. I need to get lost. I need to know someone cares. I don't want a drink. I want to fuck. I need to feel something. You have three seconds to say no."

He bites my bottom lip and tugs. "Yes."

That's all he needs. He pulls my tank over my head and growls when he sees the piercing through my left nipple. He grabs it with his teeth and pulls. The combination of pleasure and pain sends my body into overdrive. I tear at the button of his jeans. I pull at his shirt. I'm desperate. I rub my thighs together, trying to get some relief.

He pulls away long enough to take his shirt off and then his lips are on me. His tongue plunges into my mouth, an explosion of mint and pure Harley. I pinch the barbell through his nipple and he growls. He shoves me into the living room, hot on my heels. As he pushes me onto the couch, he yanks my pajama bottoms off. This isn't going to be gentle. This isn't going to be making love or having sex. This is pure anger, pure adrenaline, pure carnal fucking need.

Our breathing echoes through the room. It's dark but I can sense his every move. I hear his zipper and the rustling of the rest of his clothes coming off. My body is on fire. Every part of me is screaming for release, for contact. I know this is just an escape for him. I'm a substitute for drinking tonight. I warn my heart not to get involved but I'm a few months too late. Harley owned part of my heart the first night I met him.

He pushes me down into the cushions, the weight of his body on mine is heaven. My hands run down the length of his back. Every inch of him is covered in muscle and I shiver. He's gorgeous and he's mine, if only for a few hours.

His fingers run through my folds and I'm instantly drenched. "Jesus, Laney. You're soaked."

As he slides a finger into me, I moan long and low. I clench around him and his eyes hood. "That feels good." I bite my lip as he makes eye contact with me.

His forehead comes down and rests on mine. His finger circles lazily over my clit, starting that slow burn that I've been craving. "I'm nervous, Laney." He laughs. "I've never done this with anyone else."

"I'll be gentle." I push him onto the couch next to me and lick down his chest, his perfect abs, the drool worthy V, to his thick erection. My mouth waters as I lick the drops off the tip of his hard cock. He moans as I circle the head and I smile. "Let me make you forget for a little while."

I watch him closely for any clues that this is too much, too soon. When he tips his head back in pleasure, I keep going. I run my tongue up his length and take him into my mouth completely. When he hits the back of my throat, I hum and suck hard. He hisses and his eyes widen. When they lock with mine, I know this is ok.

He tangles his hands into my hair and whispers my name. "Laney."

It is the most beautiful sound I've ever heard. My hands caress his balls then press on the sensitive spot just behind them. His back bows and my pace quickens, my mouth warm and wet, begging for his release.

His breathing changes and I smile to myself. I've helped him after the betrayal today. If only for a little bit, the old Harley is back. I miss him.

"Stop." He gasps for breath, eyes closed, concentration written all over his face. "Holy shit. I need a minute."

His fingers caress my face and he smiles. His brown eyes are even darker with desire and I'm shaking with need. I need him to feel good. I need to finish. I'm in desperate need of an orgasm.

As if he can read my mind, his finger trails over my breasts, down my stomach and stops right where I need him most. His touch is gentle, slowly torturing me. When I whimper, he smiles at me. "What do you want, Laney?"

My heart pounds out of my chest. "I want you."

He leans forward and pulls on my bottom lip with his teeth. "You'll get me. What do you want?"

"I want you to feel good. I want you to forget." It's a risk but I need him to know I'm ok with whatever happens tonight.

He brings his fingers to his mouth and moans. "I need more of that."

He pushes me onto my back on the living room floor and dives between my legs. His tongue plunges into my core, his fingers circling my clit, his moans bringing me close to orgasm. When his tongue finds my swollen bundle of nerves, I scream his name. My body explodes, my toes curl, and pleasure pours from my body. He continues to lap at my clit until every spasm subsides.

He leans up, centering himself over me and takes a deep breath. "Please tell me you're on the pill. I can't stop."

When I nod my head yes, that's all the encouragement he needs.

Chapter 7

This is it. The moment of truth. The moment I can't take back for as long as I live. I take a deep breath. Laney's so beautiful. Her eyes shine with love, her body begs for more. Can I live with myself if I go through with this? Della's gone. Della's gone. It's been almost six months. This isn't a forever thing. I will never love anyone like I loved her. I need to feel wanted. I need to feel love.

I want this. The way my heart is pounding tells me everything I need to know. I trust Laney more than almost anyone in the world. She's a straight shooter, tell it like it is, live life to the fullest, kind of girl. She's exactly who I can take this next step with.

I lean down and kiss her once more. Our tongues meet in a passionate dance and I can't help myself. I push into her slowly, her tight, hot walls squeezing me. Holy shit. I could lose it right now and I haven't even started to move. I didn't know it would feel this good. I feel the sweat break out across my forehead.

"Laney." She opens her eyes and looks at me. "I can't offer you anything other than this. If I need to stop, please stop me now. In a minute, I won't be able to."

She leans up onto her elbows and her body clenches around me. She's soaked and I slip in even further. "Don't you dare stop."

I circle my hips and my cock hits her G-spot. She cries out and I can't help but smirk. She's so responsive and it pushes me further. I want to hear her scream again. It's all I can think about.

I grab her hair, pulling her head back and suck on her neck as I pound into her. Her tits bounce against me and I swear I get harder. I can feel every stroke hit the spot that is driving her wild. Her head thrashes back and forth and her back bows off the floor.

"Fuck me harder, Harley." Her legs wrap around my waist and for a second, I get butterflies in my stomach.

I pull almost all the way out and shove back in. Her whole body contracts around mine. I do it again. And again. Fuck! The need to come is overwhelming. I try to control my breathing. I circle my hips and my pelvis rubs her clit. She grabs my ass and grinds against me.

"I'm going to come, Laney." I pant against her lips. "Fuck. Your pussy feels so good."

Just like that, she throws her head back and screams my name. One more stroke and I empty myself into her. Our orgasms mingle together and cover both of us. I'm soaked. I'm completely sated. I'm almost happy for a few minutes.

"Shit." I collapse on top of her. I can't catch my breath. "That was so good. Shit."

She reaches up and cups my cheeks. "Are you ok?"

Am I ok? I take a deep breath and let myself feel. I almost slept with Oksana, who killed my fucking wife. I trusted my life and the life of the woman I loved to the man I thought was family, who killed my fucking wife. I want a drink almost as bad as I want to fuck Laney again. Another deep breath. And another. The hole in my heart doesn't seem as big as it did a few hours ago.

I look into Laney's bright eyes. I see a mixture of fear and desire. When she smiles at me, another part of my walls crumble.

I smile at her. "You know what, Lane? I think I'm ok tonight."

I wake to the smell of bacon. There isn't a smell more alluring than bacon being cooked first thing in the morning. I can hear Laney moving around in the kitchen and I wait for the guilt to hit me. The only problem is that it never does. I keep taking deep breaths, waiting for it. I'm not sure what it means but it scares the shit out of me.

I stretch. Sleeping on the couch is torture on my back. I groan when my knees pop. I feel like I'm a thousand years old. Sleeping next to Laney would have been better on my weary body but my heart wouldn't allow that. We took things to a whole new level last night but I was completely honest about what it meant. Wasn't I? Shit, now I don't know. I enjoyed it so much more than I expected to.

"Shit." I rub the sleep from my eyes and look around for my shirt. I find all my things folded nicely on the coffee table.

"You're awake." Laney takes a big gulp of coffee. Fuck, she looks good in the morning.

It's not guilt that hits me. It's panic. I can't get out of here fast enough. I grab my jeans and pull them on. My heart's pounding like I just got caught doing something I shouldn't have.

"Are you ok?" Her big blue eyes captivate me and I freeze for a minute. She raises her eyebrows and waits for my answer.

"Good." Shit. That answer was not only way too fast but I sounded like a teenager going through a voice change. I clear my throat. "I'm good. Are you good?"

"Harley, sit down." When I don't, she puts her hands on her hips. It's a battle of wills but she'll win. She's too calm. Christ, she's gorgeous.

I sit down on the couch and lean forward to rest my forearms on my knees. "I'm sitting."

Laney's forehead wrinkles. "Why are you sweating? Are you panicking?"

I can't help but chuckle. The girl's always been a straight shooter. "Is it that obvious?"

"Yes." She takes another sip of coffee and licks a drip off the side of the mug.

Griffin Jr. is now completely awake. Traitorous bastard. I shift uncomfortably on the couch. She notices right away and she fights her smile. "I don't think last night was a mistake. At least, I don't think I do. I'm not sure why I'm panicking. It's also really hot in here. And my back is killing me."

I'm a fucking idiot. What the hell is wrong with me? I'm never nervous. I'm pretty sure I've completely lost my mind. I reach into my pants pocket and take out a handful of Red Hots and throw them all into my mouth at once. That was a mistake. Now I'm sweating even harder. Where the fuck are my shoes?

"Hey." She touches my shoulder and I jump. "If you need to go, it's ok. I don't expect anything if that's what you're worried about. Last night was amazing but I understand what it was. I'm always here for you if you need anything."

I'm off the couch and grabbing my shoes before she even finishes her sentence. Do I kiss her goodbye? I've never had a one night stand and proper protocol is completely unclear here. I'm not even going to put on my shoes. I'll do it outside. I need air.

"Thank you for last night." I take a huge breath. "That makes me sound like a total douche."

Laney laughs. "It's ok. I know what you meant. Do you need a ride home?"

I point to the door. Why am I pointing at the door? I'm pretty sure she knows where her door is. "I'm going to go. I'll walk. The fresh air will do me good."

"Ok." She smiles. "And, Harley?"

I stop on the porch but I can't turn around. "Yeah?"

"Thanks for letting me be the person you turned to."

I close the door behind me and grab my cell phone. My hands are shaking as I dial. I'm giving up hope but on the third ring, she finally answers. "I need you."

Chapter 8

I take the stairs two at a time. I need to see her. I need to confess everything. No one will understand what I did better than she will. And she's never passed any judgment on me.

The waiting room is empty but I still pace impatiently. Last night, Laney was exactly what I needed. I don't regret a single second. I was sure I'd wake up feeling completely guilty. The only thing that makes me feel bad is the thought of driving her away.

"I'm glad you called me." Rachel is always a sight for sore eyes. When the label hired her to help us through Della's loss, I fought against her. I didn't want to talk and I sure as shit didn't want help. But there's something about Rachel. Something draws you in and actually makes you want to talk to her. Her eyes are almost gray and completely forgiving. She's soft like Della was. She's pretty without effort, her heart is huge and open, and her smile is calming.

"I didn't know who else to call." I hug her before walking into her office and taking a seat in her oversized recliner.

"Griffin, I've told you a million times that you can call me anytime. As a friend or a counselor. Whichever you need at that time." She sits down and grabs her pad of paper. "I'm here for you."

"I know." I take a minute and try to organize my thoughts. I'm not even sure how to start this conversation.

"How many drinks have you had today?" Right to the point.

"None today. None last night."

"Have you wanted to drink today?" I wait for the judgment but it doesn't come.

"All day." It's the truth. I pull some more Red Hots from my pocket. "I slept with Laney."

Her eyes widen and her lips curl at the corner. "How do you feel about that?"

"I don't know. I feel like shit that I don't feel like shit. I've never been with anyone but Dell. I'm pissed at myself for not feeling guilty."

"Why do you think you should feel guilty?"

"I cheated on Della. Sort of. Did I? Shit. I don't know. It's been six months and I was with her more than half my life. That seems fast."

Rachel puts the pad and paper down. "Do you want my answer as a friend? Or as your therapist?"

I chuckle. "Give me both, Doc."

"As your therapist, I would ask you if you feel like you were just looking for a distraction other than taking a drink. I would ask you if you were replacing the alcohol for sex and then I'd ask if you were going to do it again. I would ask you why you felt you were cheating and I'd ask more in depth questions about that." Rachel leans forward and takes my hand. "As your friend, I would say you've had one hell of a week and I think Laney is exactly the person to turn to if you're going to turn to anyone. I'm proud of you for not feeling worse. It could have been a disaster and ruined your friendship. It doesn't seem like it will. And judging by the smile you got on your face when you told me, I'd say it was probably a good move."

"I can't offer her a relationship. I was really clear about that. I'm just afraid I'll hurt her anyway." That's my biggest fear. Through it all, Laney has been a constant in the house and in our plans when we go somewhere as a group. She's not only Mia's best friend. She was a companion when I first lost Dell. She'd sit with me and let me cry or scream or tear up the house. She'd never say anything or interrupt me. She just let me be me and I needed someone who would do that.

"Della's gone, Griff. She'd never expect you to stop living. I know that's so easy to say when you aren't going through it. The truth of the matter is that someday, you're going to want to move on with your life. It may not be now. It may not be years from now. But someday, I promise, you will look around at your life and realize you're ready to move on. And it's ok to do that. She's not here to give you permission but in your heart, I know you know she'd want that."

My breath comes out in a huge whoosh. I feel like I've been holding my breath for six months. "I know she'd want me to be happy. She'd kick my ass knowing I'm drinking and being a first class asshole. I just can't stop. I can't let myself open up to Laney or anyone. I can't imagine living with someone that isn't Dell. I know it's ok if I move on. I just can't."

"You are the only person that can make the changes that need to happen. You're the only one who has the power in your life. Your friends are enabling you to continue on this destructive path. They're so afraid to lose you too that they're just ignoring the elephant in the room. They're all grieving Della's death but more than that, they're grieving losing you."

"I'm selfish."

"No, Harley, you're human." Rachel smiles at me. "We all grieve in different ways. Some of us get depressed, some of us find comfort in denial and some of us get angry at the world. You fought hard to get your alcohol addiction under control in the past. It isn't a surprise that you've turned back to alcohol. You'll always be an addict. But you need to make a decision. Is your life worth anything to you anymore?"

I know what has to be done but I don't think I'm strong enough. I stare out the window and watch the city in the background. There's life out there and it's painful to see. But, for the first time in six months, I wonder if that life is worth taking a risk on.

"We have six more stops. I owe the band that much." I'm kidding myself. There's no way I can make it through the next two weeks without taking a drink. She's not buying it either. "What if you come with us?"

"And do what, exactly? Stalk you twenty-four hours a day smacking the drinks out of your hand? You have to want this." And for just a minute, I feel judged.

"I do want this. I don't want a keeper, Rachel. If I wanted that, I would have looked up my father. I just need someone that will be there to cheer me on if I succeed. Or pick me back up if I fail." My voice is harsh and I instantly regret it. She's here to help me see the truth. It's not something I like to see. "Sorry."

"Don't apologize. I'm happy to see some fire back in that spirit. If the guys are ok with it, I'll be happy to head out on tour with you. But I want complete honesty. I want to know when you want a drink or I want to see you immediately if you have one. Can you do that?" She puts her hand out and I take it.

I've just made a deal with the devil.

Chapter 9

I haven't heard much from Harley since they went back out on tour. The first week went by quickly. I dove into work and did everything I could to ignore the voice in my head that kept reminding me to think about him. I promised myself I wouldn't let my heart get involved. The second he walked into my house, I knew I was being used. I was completely ok with that. Now that I've gotten a taste of Harley Miles, I want more.

"Stop dragging ass. We're going to be late." Mia drags my suitcase down to the waiting limo. "I haven't seen Damien in a week. Let's go."

"You're a moody bitch when you aren't getting any." She sticks her tongue out at me. "Real mature, Mia."

"Get your ass in the car." She points into the backseat and I salute her with my middle finger as I get in.

"I didn't even know there was anywhere to play in Bakersfield." I grab a bottle of water and settle in for the short drive.

"I'm glad you're coming with me. It's more fun with you there. Besides, I don't know Rachel that well. I didn't want to go with them since I knew she'd be on the bus with Harley. It felt like I was intruding."

I haven't told anyone about me and Harley. I can't. I feel like it would be a betrayal somehow. It's a good memory and I don't want to share it. Her announcement about Rachel stings for a minute. "Why's Rachel with them?"

Mia shrugs her shoulders. "Harley's trying to get clean. He asked her to go with him and watch him I guess. Damien says he's doing pretty well. He's had two nights that he was drinking and D says that one of them was stopped early. I guess once he took his first drink, he went and found her and asked her to take it away. He's trying and I'm really proud of him."

I smile. "I am too."

"Why are you smiling like that?" Mia puts her drink down and moves to sit next to me. "Spill it."

"Spill what? I'm proud of him. I was there the night he got glass in his legs. I've seen him at his worst. It will be nice to see sober Harley again."

She's staring at me. That's ok. Stare all you want. I'm not giving anything up. If I never have him again, no one can take away the one night that I did.

That seemed to appease her. Mia grabs her phone and starts sending texts to Damien. Never in a million years did I picture a day when I'd be in a limo on the way to see Liquid Regret with the fiancé of the lead singer. I never imagined I would consider these men my friends. They're nothing like I imagined they'd be. For the first time on the trip, butterflies take flight in my stomach. Not only am I heading out to see my favorite band, I'm doing it in style. My life it good.

The arena is starting to buzz. I love the feeling before a concert. The crowd is vibrating with excitement. There's anticipation, there's lust, there's an adrenaline rush like no other. We got about ten minutes backstage before Joshua told us it was time to go. I got to talk to Max but the rest of the men were in their dressing rooms with the doors closed.

Max is the biggest surprise of the band. I used to think his lack of media attention was because he was shy. That's not even close. He's wild, his laugh is contagious and loud and he loves to embarrass the other guys. He's called the mystery of the group because he stays off social media, hides from the paparazzi, and basically leads a life behind closed doors. I've never heard about a love interest and definitely haven't heard about his family. He keeps his secrets locked down and his walls are impenetrable. It's what makes Max, Max.

Chance is a little harder to bond with. He's nice and personable but his desire to look through me is an issue. When we first met, he used his legendary 'take a chance on me' pick up line. We laughed like hell that night. When Mia left the bar with Damien, I was left with Chance and Max. I suppose my rejection is what made him look through me. He's hot and if he weren't a rock star, I would have gone home with him. I just couldn't picture myself in the long line of groupies in his life. He's got the reputation as the lady's man of the group. I just didn't want to be one of his ladies.

I have to admit, I'm intrigued by Joshua. He's completely bad ass. He doesn't take anyone's shit, including mine. And believe me, I've tried to shovel it his way just to see how far I can push him. The answer is, I can't. He doesn't give me a second look. I asked Harley once if he thought Joshua might be gay. He just laughed at me. Turns out, he used to be married but his wife couldn't handle the long weeks out on the road. He swore off women, saying they were nothing but grief. I can't wait for him to fall in love. Watching the great Joshua Seymour fall to his knees for a woman will be worth all the yelling and ugly looks he gives all of us.

The lights dim and the crowd starts to scream. I can't help but join in. I grab Mia's hand and we jump up and down with all the rest of the women who are going crazy for just a glimpse of these rock gods. I'm so excited that I can't help but giggle. They might be my friends but they put on an incredible show and I turn into a screaming fan and get lost in the music.

The drum beat starts and I shiver. Max is pounding out the beat and laser lights go crazy. More screaming. Then the bass guitar joins. Chance matches the rhythm set by Max as the lights reflect off the four stringed guitar. Smoke rises from the stage and all I can see are their shadows but I'd be able to tell them apart anywhere. Harley takes a few steps forward and the first chord from his six string sends the crowd into overdrive. The screams are piercing and I can't help but smile. He's in his element and he's happy.

Without Novocain starts and the crowd sings along as Damien's voice echoes through the theater. The lights come up and I get the chills.

They're all smiling as they play the song that landed them on the top of the charts. Max's voice sings harmony as they get to the chorus. They're perfect and I'm completely mesmerized.

Damien dances across the stage like he's in a trance. Chance and Harley lean into each other as they let the music take them away. The energy from the crowd is addicting and I dance along with the rest of the front row.

When the first song is over, Harley steps forward and throws his guitar pick into the audience. The girls go crazy and he laughs. Blowing them a kiss, he scans the front row. He's surprised when he sees me and I panic for one split second. It's all forgotten when he points at me and yells my name with a laugh.

I get 'the look' from Mia but I just shrug. She puts her arm around me and laughs. "Whatever you're doing, keep doing it."

She yells into my ear but I'm already lost watching Harley. What happened between us hasn't changed anything. That's the best news I've had all week.

Chapter 10

This crowd is intense. I rarely ever wear my ear monitor but thank God I have it tonight. The noise in the arena is insane. I push the monitor further into my ear. It won't help but it's a nervous habit I have when we play for a full house. I've seen Damien mess with his about six times during our three minute song. I send a silent prayer up to the rock gods and lose myself in the song.

I can feel Chance at my back. I lean into him and close my eyes. It feels good to be back on stage. It's what I needed. It gives me purpose and routine. I need this if I'm going to stop drinking and start believing I'm worth it.

A smile creeps onto my face. All the bullshit fades away. I chomp my cinnamon gum and feel the burn. I've eaten so many Red Hots in the last week that it's possible I've burnt a hole in my stomach. It's keeping me from getting wasted. I had one night of weakness and the look on Rachel's face the next morning made me feel like shit. Two days later, I picked up a beer, took one sip and went out in search of forgiveness. She gave it to me without having to ask.

As the song comes to an end, I step to the edge of the stage and throw the first of many guitar picks at the screaming women in the first few rows. There's always a scuffle and I can't help but laugh when one of the girls almost takes her friend out trying to get to it.

I can feel the sweat drip down my back from the hot stage lights. I grab a pick from my pocket and scan the front row. One of the best parts of my job is watching the way the crowd reacts to us. There's so much energy to feed off of. I'm alive and I'm ok tonight.

I see Mia screaming and watching Damien. It makes me laugh. My eyes catch a glimpse of the gorgeous woman standing next to her. Her eyes catch mine and it makes me feel like a superhero. I haven't had someone in the audience for me since Della died. She's here because she wants to be not because I'm paying her to listen to my bullshit. She's here because she loves this band and that's a huge fucking revelation. I feel supported and loved. For the first time in forever, I don't feel alone.

"Laney." I point to her and yell her name. The smile she gives me makes my heart jump.

What the fuck was that? I shake it off and start the next song on our playlist. We took the song that Damien wrote for Mia when he asked her to marry him and turned it into a masterpiece. The women swoon when we play it and I can feel the eyes of every pissed off man in the room. Not our fault that Damien is whipped and came up with something romantic for his woman.

Each song flows into the next. I'm exhausted and covered in sweat. This is what I'm living for now. I know that Della is with us every night when we take the stage. I feel her when I play, I feel her when I let the music take over, I feel her when I'm done with a show and I feel like I've run a marathon.

I also know that she's with me in the quiet moments. Rachel finds nature healing and I just go with it. She's trying to remind me that I'm still alive and I know her job is hard. She's working through all my bullshit and I know that can't be easy. When we sit outside and I talk about how much I love Della, I feel her in the breeze. Rachel never tells me I'm crazy for that. It's probably just a coincidence but every time I start to miss her and blame myself or start to feel bad, the wind picks up and reminds me that I'm just a tiny part of the big picture. Yesterday, we talked about Laney. As soon as I said that I thought I should feel horrible for what I did, the wind picked up. Rachel smiled but I couldn't help but cry like a fucking baby.

I felt like it was an ok from the woman that changed my entire life. It felt like permission to be happy and the weight of the world shifted off my shoulders. Pieces of my heart started to mend and some of my guilt blew away in the breeze. I've spent every second of the last six months thinking about Della or searching for ways to forget. In that one second, I realized I could still love her the way I do and have a life again.

It'll be a long time before I love again. And if it happens, it'll never be the same kind of love I had with Dell. What we had was once upon a lifetime. I gave my heart to her the first day I met her. The second I looked at her, she owned me. I'm scared she always will.

When the lights go down for our last song, I step to the front of the stage.   My fingers throb, I'm overheated, I'm happy. I'm fucking happy and I don't know what to do with that. Rachel's going to have a field day with me tomorrow.

"You were amazing." Her voice is like balm to my aching body.

I open my eyes and smile at her. I'm completely exhausted but I need to be near her. I pat the sofa next to me. The dressing room is small and plain but it gives me privacy and somewhere to relax. When I feel the cushion next to me dip, I lean into her.

"I didn't know you were coming. It was a nice surprise to see you in the audience." I can't help but yawn.

"You should get some sleep."

I don't know where she thinks she's going. I grab her hand. "Stay."

She smiles at me before sitting back down. "I wasn't sure how you'd react after the other night. I'm glad you aren't still panicking."

Her laugh makes me laugh. "I freaked out."

"A little." She leans her head onto my shoulder and the smell of her shampoo hits me. It's exclusively Adelaine Jones. I've never smelled anything like it and I'll never be able to forget it.

"I've been working with Rachel for the last week. When I left your place, I went right to her office. I don't want to get into all the deep shit but I panicked for nothing. Thanks for not rubbing it in." I can't help but chuckle. I really was an idiot that morning.

I can hear Chance and Damien messing around out on stage. Nights like this remind me this is truly a family. When backstage is quiet, we sneak back out on stage and practice new songs or just mess around with different riffs. There've been times we've even convinced Joshua to pick up a mic and join us. I smile when I hear the blaring music.

"Come with me." I grab Laney's hand and pull her behind me. When we get to the side of the stage, I notice the speaker set up for the sound crew. Chance's bass vibrates through the back hall. I put my hand on the speaker and give Laney an evil grin.

"That's a look I haven't seen before." She cocks an eyebrow at me.

"Come here." I'm not asking. I point to the speaker.

She comes to me, confusion written all over her face. It's replaced by shock when I spin her around and bend her over the speaker. I kick her legs apart and lean down over her back. My tongue runs up her neck. "Do you trust me?"

She shivers and pushes her perfect ass into me. Game on. I have her dress pulled up around her waist and her panties torn off before she has a chance to make a sound. She's already dripping and it's the hottest thing I've ever seen. Could we be caught here? Absolutely. It just makes it more exciting.

Chance wails on his guitar and the speaker vibrates hard. Laney whimpers as I rock her into it. This is going to be more fun than I thought.

I'll have to thank Chance later. For now, I need to be buried inside her.

I wait for Chance to blast another note. When he does, I shove into her and she screams my name. Her legs shake, the constant vibration of the speaker driving her closer and closer. Her walls are squeezing me and I know I won't last long. Her body was made for fucking and at this moment, I'm the luckiest son of a bitch on the planet.

Her nails dig into my arms and I feel her whole body tighten before she shatters, soaking my cock. I don't even let her come down from the first orgasm. My pounding is relentless as I race toward ecstasy.

Chapter 11

Laney

Holy fuck. I thought the first time was good. This time is complete bliss. The speaker vibrates against my clit and I can't help but grind against it. Harley's cock fills me and at this angle, he's so deep that I want to scream in pleasure.

Chance picks up speed and causes the speaker to vibrate harder. I start to pant. I'm so close. I dig my nails into Harley's arms. I need to hold on. Pleasure builds and builds. My body goes rigid as I fall over the edge. The orgasm is the hardest I've ever had. Light explodes behind my eyes and for a minute, I feel like I could pass out.

"That's it, baby." Harley pounds into me from behind and a second orgasm starts in my toes. "Again."

I shake my head no. There's no way. The pleasure is too much. His strokes get faster and harder. "I can't. It's too much. I can't."

"You can and you will." He grabs my hair and pulls. The pain shoots straight to my core. Damien screams a note on stage and my clit vibrates hard. Harley pushes me into the speaker and grinds against me.

My orgasm hits without warning and I explode all over Harley's cock. The force of it almost pushes him out of me. My whole body spasms as he's right there with me.

His body collapses on top of me. "Laney," he breathes against my neck as he fills me with heat. The speaker continues to vibrate and with him on top of me, my clit is buried against it. Another orgasm starts to build deep in my belly. I gasp and try to move but he won't let me go.

"You've got another one in there. I need to feel it. I want it all over me. Give it to me, Lane." His breath in my ear makes me shiver.

Before I can respond, another wave of pleasure tears through me and I scream his name. I can't hold back any longer. My whole body shakes in pleasure. I can't take any more. "Please. No more."

"I say when it's enough." He pushes up and starts to move again. I can feel him getting hard again.

I whimper. It feels so good and my body is like a live wire. I go completely limp on top of the speaker.

The stage goes dark and I instantly miss the extra attention my clit was getting. I'm insatiable with him. My body has never responded the way it does when he's buried inside me.

I cry out his name as another wave hits me. It's too much. It's not nearly enough. I don't care if this is temporary. He needs it and honestly, so do I. It feels so fucking good and I don't ever want it to stop. That thought scares the shit out of me.

I feel completely boneless as Harley leads me out to say goodbye to everyone. The new security guard at the backstage door smiles at me. I don't remember his name but he stayed near us during the concert to make sure we were ok. He's holding a girl back that is causing quite the scene. I roll my eyes and think it must be hell to have people throwing themselves at the guys. I giggle. Isn't that what I just did? Oh my God. I'm a groupie.

"I want to see Cal. This is insane. He'll want to see me." The woman is perfectly manicured and too groomed to be your average groupie. "Tell him Morgan is here."

"Ma'am. Max is already on the tour bus. It's time to go."

"Max." She practically spits his name. "Go get him."

"Give me just a second." Harley squeezes my hand before walking over to the security guard. "Is there a problem?"

"Yes there is." She glares at Harley. "I drove all the way here from Newport Beach and I'm not leaving until I speak to Callum. We grew up in Newport together. He'll want to see me."

Harley's forehead wrinkles. "I think you have him confused with someone else. Max isn't a Newport native."

This bitch actually has the nerve to touch Harley. I step forward before I realize what I'm doing. She might look perfect but I can take her. Newport Beach meet the streets of LA. I've got this. 'Hey blondie. Remove your hands from my property."

Harley flinches. I didn't mean it how it came out. But no one touches someone important to me. He won't make eye contact with me. I'll handle that later.

"I just want to talk to Callum." Bombshell Barbie looks defeated.

"Morgan?" Max's voice is hardly a whisper.

"Callum Maxwell. It's been a long time."

"How did you find me?" Max's face goes completely pale.

"The little media stunt with the red head didn't keep you very hidden. Can we talk?" Morgan follows a confused Max down the hall. Before they shut the door, his eyes meet mine. His look is a mixture of fear and heartbreak. I have an intense desire to protect him.

"What just happened?" My eyes are wide when I look at Harley.

"Make sure no one gets in that room." Harley's voice is stern and the bodyguard jumps into gear. "Don't even let Seymour in there. No one."

He pulls me down the hall and it's hard to keep up. "Slow down."

Harley slams his dressing room door. "What the hell was that? Jesus, Laney. Please tell me I didn't just fuck up backstage. Please tell me I was clear about what the sex actually means."

"Calm your shit, Miles. I know what we are and I know what being together means. It pissed me off that she touched you like that. She was pissed and no one gets to touch any of you in anger. Especially not some princess from Newport Beach." Why am I so angry? The words were out of my mouth before I knew what I was saying. It was wrong to imply Harley's mine. I knew it the second he pulled away. "I'm sorry. I thought she was just a crazy fan trying to get back to you guys."

He tucks a strand of hair behind my ear. The gesture is intimate and sends my heart into overdrive. I'm completely screwed. "Thank you. And for the record, not sure I want to fuck with badass Laney."

I feel my inner slut rear her horny head. "Don't fuck *with* me. But I hope you still want to fuck me."

He growls. "I'm not sure I'll be able to get enough of fucking you, Lane. Your body was made for fucking and I plan on fucking the hell out of it."

I shiver. "Prove it."

"Be careful what you wish for Ms. Jones." Just as his lips meet mine, there's a knock at the door and Rachel calls his name. He closes his eyes and takes a deep breath. "Fuck."

Harley opens the door and Rachel looks past him to where I'm standing. Her eyes widen and she looks back at Harley. "Have you had a drink?"

Harley's hands ball into fists. "No."

"Are you trading one addiction for another?" She winks at me. I know she's trying to help him but that stung a little.

"Sex is a healthier addiction. I can't get hurt fucking." Harley chuckles. "Well, maybe I can but a hard on is better than a hangover."

"Poetic, Griff." She pats him on the shoulder. "I got a text from

Max. He needs to talk so I'll be in his dressing room. Knock if you need me. You are my first priority."

"Sorry." Harley looks at me with sympathetic eyes. "She obviously knows about us. I promised to be completely honest."

"Honest. Hmm." I wonder if he'll buy the innocent act. "What's going on with Max? What did she call him? Callum Maxwell?"

"You like him." His smile is evil. "Should I be worried?"

I can't help but clap. "Excellent deflection, Mr. Miles. Excellent."

Chapter 12

The fact that I actually feel jealous of Max is a huge problem. It's not like I'm having a big relationship with Laney. I would say we aren't any more than the dreaded friends with benefits. So why am I worried about her feelings for Max?

The last week on tour flew by. Before we knew it, we were back in LA making plans to record the next album. As soon as we got back, I moved out of Damien's. I appreciate all they've done for me but it's torture watching them developing what Della and I had together. I vowed to start moving on. First step, finding a new place to start over. Max is more than happy to have the company while I'm looking.

Since the first clue of his real identity came to light in a way we weren't ready for, I actually feel better being here with him. I'm not worried about his safety, just his sanity. When the true "Max" is finally revealed, shit may hit the fan. I'd like to be by his side when that happens. He's always been here for me.

He's in the middle of his living room working out with a personal trainer and I can't help but watch him. I suppose if I was a woman, I'd find him good looking. Hell, he's tall, blond, very boy next door looking. No tattoos, no piercings, just plain ole Max. I can see what Laney would see in him. Add to it the fact that he's not fucked in the head and it makes him a much better man for her. Of course, now that I've seen Morgan, I'm not sure two toned hair, pierced nipple, tatted Laney is really his type. She's got that adorable bow tattooed on her thigh. He better not fucking know about that tattoo.

"Max, tell me about Laney's tattoos." What the fuck am I doing? Have I turned into a complete pussy?

"What the hell for?" Max wipes his forehead with his towel and gives me a look that makes me laugh.

"Just my subtle attempt at asking how many you know about."

Max's forehead wrinkles. "About as subtle as a gun, bro. She's got a tattoo on her left arm from the elbow down. She's got something tattooed on the back of both her legs. Oh, and the little heart right above her.."

"Bullshit.   There's no tattoo there." Hook, line and sinker. Busted.

"I fucking knew it." Max belly laughs. "Something you want to tell me?"

"Not really.   Just wondering how well you actually know each other."

Max sits across from me at the breakfast bar. "I adore Lane. She's great. But there are two issues with our relationship. She sees me as a brother and it's not her pussy I want to get lost in."

I'm intrigued.   Morgan was pretty hot, in a bitchy, arrogant way. It would be fun to break her ass down in the sack. "Good to hear."

Max just nods before he takes another sip of water. "Now you know something, too. Bro code, man."

I fist bump him as he walks out of the kitchen. It's nice to see Max back in the saddle. It's been awhile and I'd love to see him happy. And this time, with anyone other than the girl that I... Wait, no. What the fuck was that? If my heart and brain don't get on the same page, I'm going to have to walk away. There's no way I'll let those bastards fight each other. If my heart won, I'd never forgive myself.

Especially not now. Tomorrow would have been Della's thirty-first birthday. I know when I wake up tomorrow, my heart is going to be ripped out all over again. The thought of that makes me reach for the cinnamon candy in my pocket. It's twenty-four hours. I'm going to need Rachel tomorrow. I'm not strong enough to handle this on my own. Not her birthday. Not yet.

Fuck! I can't breathe. It's like it's happening all over again. It's pouring outside and I can't imagine it's an accident. I hope Oksana and Lex are rotting away in jail. If there is justice in this world, I hope Lex is somebody's bitch by now. If he ever sees the light of day again, I'll make him mine.

"It's been more than six months." My voice is barely a whisper. "I miss you so much."

Her gravestone stares back at me. I haven't been here since the day we put her in the ground. The thought of knowing I'll never see her again is overwhelming. The desperation is pulling me under and my only salvation is in the bottle of amber liquid in my pocket. I'm not strong enough to face this world without her. I'm too lonely and too weak.

I run my fingers over the cold bottle. It'll all be over if I just unscrew the cap. My brain is screaming 'don't do this'. I should call Rachel. She's the only one that can stop me but it'll be too late. The liquor is my friend. I text her in hopes that will make me stronger but it only makes me feel worse.

I unscrew the top and fall to my knees at the headstone. "I'm so sorry, Della." I put the bottle to my lips and moan as the liquid burns my throat.

The minute the liquor hits me, I feel alive. I know the crash is coming but I don't care. I chug half the bottle without breathing. My tears are flowing as fast as the liquor. I reach out and rub my fingers over the words on the headstone. Beloved wife.

"Della." I lie down knowing that she's right below me. If I could get to her, I'd dig through this dirt with my bare hands. "I'm so sorry I wasn't there. I was supposed to protect you and I couldn't. I let them both into our lives and they stole what mattered most. I would take your place if I could. I'm so sorry."

The rain is cold and soaks through my clothes. I'm shivering. I deserve the punishment and welcome it with open arms. The more I drink, the more I don't care. The bottle is almost empty and I throw it on the grass next to me. I can't take back what I've done. Sitting up, I rest my back against the cold granite that now defines my wife's life. How did life even get to this? I close my eyes and welcome the sting of the raindrops on my face.

"Harley." I hear them coming and I don't care. It's done. My head spins and it's hard to pick it up to even look at them.

Rachel kneels in front of me and puts her hands on my cheeks. "I need you to get up. You're going to get sick if you stay out here."

"I don't care." I close my eyes but she shakes me to make me look at her again.

"There has to be a part of you that cares. You sent me a message. You wanted help, Griff. Let us get you home." Her voice is sweet. I know I've let her down.

I shake my head. "I didn't want to. I had to. I can't stop. I can't live without her, Rach." My words are slurred and I'm trying so hard to let go and freefall into the darkness.

Chance is pacing. I've seen this before. It's the calm before the storm. I brace myself for impact when he makes eye contact with me.

"I've had enough of this bullshit. Where the fuck is your chip?" He's fuming.

"You aren't helping." Rachel keeps her hands on my face. They're like ice and for a second, I feel guilty for bringing her out in the rain.

"You aren't either. I'm tired of this. We're all tiptoeing around poor Harley. Your wife is dead. It fucking sucks. We all lost her. I can't watch this anymore. You need help before you kill yourself. I refuse to watch this shit. Where the fuck is your chip?" Chance crosses his arms over his chest. The water pours down the front of him and I can tell he's getting more pissed with each minute that I sit here like a victim.

"Screaming at him isn't helping." Rachel gets in his face. "Go get in the car before you say something you can't take back."

Chance leans in and the venom practically seeps from his pores. "He never goes anywhere without that chip. It took him forever to get it. The first year being sober was the hardest. He wouldn't just throw that away. He needs to remember, not sit here and drink himself into a coma."

"Back off." I know that's what I meant to say but I'm not sure it's what I actually said. My brain is in a fog and my vision is blurred. In just a few minutes, my world will go blank. I count the seconds, willing unconsciousness to take me.

Chance kneels and pulls me forward. His hands fist in my shirt and his eyes zero in on mine. "I'll ask you one more time. Where. Is. Your. Fucking. Chip?"

Complete defeat. "Della has it. I buried it with her."

"Shit!" Chance yells. "You planned to fail. You fucking planned this."

Joe, the bodyguard that has spent every second of this meltdown with me, steps forward and pushes Chance. "Get in the car." When Chance tries to pull away, Joe tightens his grip.

"I fucking begged to die." My voice cracks and I don't care. "Of course I'd fail. I don't have the only reason I was living here to keep me going."

"That's a pussy answer. You're a pussy, Griff. You'd rather die than live? Fucking do it already. Don't make the rest of us watch this anymore." Chance yells the entire way to the car. Joe shoves him in and slams the door.

Rachel pulls me in for a hug. It shocks me and I want to push her away. I don't deserve the affection. When I try to move, she holds me tighter. "The guys can't handle any more loss. They're hurting for you. They just don't know what to do."

"I don't know what to do." I can't stop myself from shaking. The tears won't stop. I'm too far gone to have any control over my body. "I need help."

Rachel sighs. "Are you ready?"

I'm terrified but I know I have two choices. I can either get some help and hope for a day that the sun rises again or say goodbye and give up living. "I'm ready."

I lean back and close my eyes as Rachel goes to talk to Joe. I take deep breaths and pray I'm doing the right thing. I haven't made the right choices for a long time. I've been selfish. I've been on a path of destruction, plowing over everyone and everything in my way.

"I'm proud of you. This is the hardest part." Rachel holds her hand out to me and I struggle to get on my feet. Her grip is strong and I know she's got me.

"Don't be yet. I've got a long way to go."

I trip three times on the way to the car. I struggle with the seatbelt as Rachel starts the car. I give up when I can't get it latched. She doesn't say anything, just gets me buckled in and smiles. I'm nauseated and cold. I know I won't stay awake for the drive. I wish I wasn't such a fuck up but I thank God that I have Rachel by my side.

"Sleep." She takes my hand. "It's a long drive. Things will look better when we get there."

As I drift off, I hear her on the phone, making reservations for where I will start the rest of my life. I send up a prayer and beg Della not to give up on me yet.

Chapter 13

    I look around the room nervously. I got a call from Max last night telling me that the guys wanted to have a meeting with everyone about their next album and other 'tour related news' as Max put it. The mood has been somber and I can't help but notice Harley is nowhere to be seen.

    As always, Max has a smile on his face. He and Rachel are talking quietly while she sips at her second cup of coffee since I've gotten here. Chance is having a heated discussion with Joshua and Damien is on his phone in the foyer. He told me Mia wasn't feeling well and was skipping the meeting.

I feel so out of place. Everyone here is a member of the band or employed by the label to counsel, protect or manage. I'm just best friend of the lead singer's fiancé. Don't get me wrong. I appreciate that they consider me a part of them. But I can't help but feel uncomfortable when the two people I'm closest to aren't here.

"I know you're all wondering why I called this meeting, so I'll make it quick. I know you have better places to be." Joshua really commands attention just by being in the room. "As you can see, Harley isn't with us this morning. Yesterday was Della's birthday and he wasn't even remotely close to being equipped to handle that. He sent Rachel a text from the cemetery that just said SOS."

My heart starts to pound and I'm frozen in fear. My mind starts racing with all the different reasons he isn't here. I look at Damien but he's just as surprised as I am. Rachel sips more coffee and I can't help the stab of jealousy that he needed someone and picked her. It's stupid and I kick myself for feeling this way.

"Chance and Rachel headed out to help him and by the time they got there, he was completely soaked and freezing. He had an entire bottle of whiskey before they got there. He's finally asked for help and Rachel drove him to Napa Valley and checked him into a rehab facility so he can get the help he needs. I know it was a long drive and you're exhausted but we'll never be able to thank you enough." Joshua smiles at Rachel and I want to jump up and hug her.

"He's in a good place and he'll get the help he needs with the privacy that he requires. He'll have phone privileges and can have visitors after the first week. If you need any other information, just let me know." Rachel looks right at me and I can't help but smile at her.

"As far as the new album goes, we'll obviously have to put that on hold. This gives us a chance to come up with more original material. The minute he's cleared to work, we need to get into the studio and lay down the tracks. We don't have a choice but to shoot the video for Betrayal this week. I know Harley and Chance were the leads but I think it's something Damien can do in Harley's place. You good with that?"

Damien smirked. "Let's see, playing a guitar, rolling around on the floor with a hot model. No, I don't think I can do that."

When Chance laughs, I'm caught off guard. He's been so angry lately and it's good to see him smiling. And the thought of Damien rolling around with anyone other than Mia makes me giggle. Her wrath is not fun to face. I've been there before and I don't want to be there again.

"We need someone edgy for the female lead. I've put out a casting call but haven't found anyone yet. Plan on being on set at six Wednesday. I know it's early but we need the entire day so let's do this without a bunch of bitching." Joshua looks right at Max. That surprises me but everyone else must know something I don't since they're all staring at him.

"What about Laney? She's edgy and has the body for it." Max smirks my way.

My face is on fire. There's no way they'd pick me to be in the video. I wish I could disappear. I hold my breath as Joshua stares at me.

"You'd be perfect. Can you act?" Joshua raises his eyebrows as he waits for my answer.

"No." I can't help but laugh. "I can learn."

"Good enough for me." Damien winks at me and I know that no matter what happens, it will be something I never forget.

"Settled. I want to thank Chance for whatever he said to Harley. I got to talk to him for a few minutes this morning and whatever you said, he heard you. With that being said, I'll get out of here so you can all have a day off. See you at 6:00 AM Wednesday." Joshua pulls his keys from his pocket.

My phone startles me awake. I reach for it and try to turn off the alarm before I realize it's ringing. It's a number I don't recognize but a call at three in the morning is never a good thing.

"Hello?" My voice cracks as I rub the sleep from my eyes.

"Laney." My heart flies into my throat.

"Harley." I smile and lie back down.

"This is an illegal call so I have to be quick." His whisper sets my body on fire.

"Are you ok?" Knowing he's sneaking out to call me makes me worry.

"I just needed to say I was sorry. I took off without saying anything to you. I felt really bad so I wanted to call you." He clears his throat. "Are we ok?"

"We're fine, Griff. It's good to hear your voice. I've been so worried."

"Lane." I can tell he wants to say something and my heart starts pounding.

"Yeah?" I whisper back.

He lets out a deep breath and I wish I could reach through the phone and hold him. I shouldn't feel this way but I do. "I need to go. I'll call again."

The phone goes dead in my hands. I picture him sweet talking a nurse to use the phone in the middle of the night. I can't help but smile. I miss him but I know he's in a good place and he needs this. We need this.

I set the phone back on the charger and pull the covers back up. As I close my eyes, I think about the night back stage and drift off to dream of the man who has stolen my heart.

"Jesus." Chance's voice scares me and I slap him in the chest as I try to get my heart to stop pounding.

"You scared the shit out of me. Why are you yelling?" My hands are shaking and it's way too early in the morning to be caked with makeup and hairspray. "Why are you staring at me?"

"You're gorgeous." Chance kisses the back of my hand. "They're waiting for you on set. I said I'd come find you since we're starting with the bedroom scene. Thought you might need a minute to freak out."

I can't help but laugh. I've had fifteen minutes with the director and just the thought of rolling around in a bed with Chance with a bunch of cameras on us makes me want to throw up. What if I'm terrible? And God only knows what I have to do with Damien.

"I see the wheels turning. What are you worried about, babe?" Chance holds my hand as we walk onto the set. "I promise it will be flawless. Honestly, I get freaked out

every time. But don't tell anyone.
I've got street cred and all that."

I can't stop myself from
laughing. It's the loud belly laugh
that Mia calls a cackle. Chance looks
at me with the strangest look on his
face before bursting into laughter
next to me.

"What the hell is that? Is that
your laugh?" Chance doesn't stop
laughing and I notice a few other
people laughing with us. "This is the
best thing I've ever heard."

"Let's go." Joshua's voice
bellows through the studio and it's
enough to send me back into heart
attack mode. "Laney and Chance,
you're up."

Damien walks over to me and
takes my hand. "Just relax and get
lost in it. They'll blast the song in the

background. It's one of our new
ones. Kind of a good versus evil
thing. Chance is the good boy that
everyone loves and you know you
shouldn't be with him. His family
would never approve. He's clean cut
and smart and successful. Think
boring." He laughs and flips Chance
the bird. "But you belong to the
tatted up bad boy from the same side
of the tracks. We're fighting for you
and in the end, you can only pick
one."

"Ok." I take a deep breath.
"Who do I pick at the end?"

"You follow your heart."
Chance smiles.

"Places!" The director yells
and we all scramble to different
spots.

As the day went on, I rolled around in the bed with Chance, who by the way, got a hard on immediately and blamed me for being hot. Even though I wanted to be shocked, I wasn't and Chance did everything he could to lighten the mood. I ran what felt like miles in a pair of stiletto boots while I held hands with Damien and tried to fight my feelings for the good boy I wasn't with. I smoked a cigarette that made me gag and want to puke. I threw stuff around in a room that was supposed to be my bedroom. I stripped down to a very small bra and almost invisible pair of panties that made me thank God I'd kept my appointment for my Brazilian earlier in the week. I learned I am amazing at crying on cue and now I'm convinced I'm in the wrong profession altogether.

I would say the day was successful. Chance and Damien seemed impressed and at the end of it all, Joshua gave me a hug and told me he couldn't have found someone more perfect for the role. It broke my heart when I found out that Damien had stepped into Harley's role. I would have loved to share this with him.

"You did a great job." Chance smiles at me as I dig through my purse for my keys. "Want to go grab a beer?"

I think about Harley. I'll never be able to explain anything to Chance. I don't want him to feel rejected and pull away again. But the last thing I want to do is lead him on. "I have to be at work super early tomorrow. I'm not able to be anything but your friend, Chance.

But if you're game for that, how about Friday night?"

"It's a date." He winks.

"It's a night out with a friend." I wink back.

Chapter 14

Every morning for the last twenty-one mornings, all the alcoholics sit in a circle in the therapy room. We're asked the same question. Why do you drink? Well, I've had all kinds of bullshit answers. The first day, it was that I liked the taste. Day two, I liked the way it made me feel. Day three, I can't sleep without it. Around day fourteen, I started to really think about the question. The honest answer is that I don't know. When it was my turn that morning, I said exactly that. To my surprise, my counselor said it was a breakthrough.

I'm not sure I would go that far. How can something be a

breakthrough when it obviously isn't an actual answer? But, it was. And it was mind blowing. There are so many layers of shit that I need to work through and this morning, I'm completely overwhelmed.

When Della died, I leaned on my old friends Jim, Jack and Jose. I thought it was so I could forget. And, in a way, it was. But I took that first drink because I was angry, scared, lonely and completely desperate. When Oksana handed me the first pill, it was the first time I felt anyone understood what I was going through. I couldn't control any part of my life except how much I drank and, before long, even that was out of my control.

"Griffin, why do you drink?" The counselor puts on his professional face and grabs that damn pen he loves so much. I'm glad I don't get to see what he actually writes.

"I drink because I feel guilty." He looks up at me and I can't stop the words pouring out of my mouth. "Guilty I wasn't there to save her. Guilty that I didn't know the person I turned to stole her from me. Guilty because she killed her because she loves me. Guilty that I'm still alive and she isn't. Guilty because I get to go on with my life and I feel like I shouldn't want to do that so soon."

"And you want to go on with your life?" When he says it, I smile at him. On the first day, I wanted to die and never thought I'd feel differently.

"Guilty because I used someone important to me to help numb the pain." I take a deep breath. This part stings. "Guilty because I feel like I cheated on my wife by using this other woman."

"If you could say one thing to Della today, what would it be?"

My eyes are burning. I try to will the tears away. "I'd say thank you for the most amazing years of my life."

He puts his pen down and looks me in the eyes. "Three weeks ago, you were too emotional to answer that question. Every other morning, you've said you were sorry. Today, you are thankful. I would say we have made some major progress, Mr. Miles."

"I would say I have a long way to go."

"Have you thought about drinking today?" Does anyone ever say no to this question and mean it?

"Every minute I've been awake." When he nods at me, I know it's someone else's turn to be tortured.

I'd like to be the cool guy, not affected by any of this. It's intensive therapy and I feel weak that I needed it. What I've learned is that so much of my addiction stems from emotional bullshit that I've swept aside thinking I was too much of a man to face it. Now I've been completely stripped naked and am vulnerable and the wounds are not only deep, they're open to so much more hurt. I have a long way to go but I'm proud of how far I've come.

"You're a sight for sore eyes." I can't help the grin on my face when I see Max. "Thanks for coming, brother."

"Three weeks too long to go without seeing my ugly mug?" Max pulls me into a hug. "How you holding up?"

"Hardest thing I've ever done." I lead him down the hallway to the community room and take a seat on the couch. "How's everything back home?"

"About the same. Chance is fucking everything that moves, Damien and Mia are planning their wedding, I've been able to dodge Morgan for a few weeks. Oh.." He pulls a DVD out. "I stole the rough copy of the video we shot. It's really good."

I take it and pop it into the DVD player. I've missed the guys. I've missed my guitar and the lack of music here is driving me insane. When the countdown starts, I feel a little sad. I was supposed to share this video with Chance and I'm painfully aware that I fucked that up. I know Damien will be great but I've never been the face of the band and I was excited about this.

"We made a couple changes but most of the script stayed the same. We hired a face you'll recognize but she fit the part better." Max offers me a piece of gum but keeps his eyes glued to the screen. "It's the best video we've shot."

"Think you'll ever put yourself into one of the videos?" When Max looks at me, I have my answer.

"Dude, you know I can't do that."

"It's going to be pretty hard to hide now. We've gotten too big to hide behind the drums forever. Maybe it's time to be Callum again?"

Max doesn't say anything, just glares at me. I know he's not ready but his cover is unravelling in front of our eyes and the shit storm that's going to come with it won't be fun.

The song starts and I look back at the video. Our director always knocks the shit out of the park and I have to say, this looks just as good as the others. Chance is in a bed, the camera zoomed in on his back. His body is moving like he's making love and the woman's nails dig into his back. It's hot and I'm wondering if there's going to be some warning so kids aren't watching it. Her legs wrap around him under the covers and I smile. The acting is almost too realistic. I imagine that Chance had her on her back after the shoot was over.

Cut to Damien and he's got her pinned against a wall. The words blare about knowing what's right but wanting what's wrong. As he lifts her arm above her head, my body stirs. Wait just a fucking minute. As he leans in and kisses her neck, the camera moves to get a side view and that two toned hair that's such a turn on is like a dagger to my heart. It's like I'm watching her cheat on me.

I start to sweat. I don't know what the hell is wrong with me. Laney isn't mine and I don't know why my body doesn't seem to understand that. When the camera cuts back to her in bed with Chance, she rolls over on top of him, her lace bra pressed against his chest. His lips drag down her neck and I can't look away. The tattoos on the back of her thighs make me hard. They're tangled in the sheets, slick with sweat, moving together in perfect harmony. I close my eyes and picture her wrapped around me, dripping, begging.

Max starts talking about the shots that they've changed and I can't even hear him. He reaches out and touches my arm and I smile.

"She's so beautiful, I can't look away. She's perfect." I see Max smile out of the corner of my eye. "What made you use Laney?"

"She was perfect. We didn't even meet with anyone else."

The video ends with Laney dressed in leather, her makeup dark and walking away from a motorcycle. Chance stands with the people hired to be his wealthy family, wearing a cap and gown and pulling away from the perfect girl next door as he runs to the girl from the wrong side of the tracks. Damien stands in the background knowing he's lost the girl and the song fades out.

I'm so turned on. Watching her with Chance and Damien was difficult but knowing it was acting helps ease the green monster that's taken ahold of my brain. The guilt I've been feeling eases as I imagine her in my lap, soaking me as she screams my name. The truth slams into me like I've been hit by a two by four. I like her more than I even realized and fucking her wasn't just to numb the pain. It was about the connection I feel with her, physically and now emotionally. I want her. My body is begging for her.

"My therapist says the best way to face my demons is to write. I've written some awesome stuff while I've been here. Give me a few minutes and I'll bring you what I've got." I stand up and pray the sweats I'm wearing don't give away how turned on I am. "I want to write something for Laney and have you take it back for me."

"Sure thing, brother. I'll grab a cup of coffee and wait in here. Take your time." Max pulls his phone from his pocket and starts to text.

I lock the door to my room and take some deep breaths. My cock throbs and my mind replays the night backstage when I drove Laney into the speaker and she came over and over and over. I reach into the waistband of my pants and fist my erection. It takes less than a minute to explode all

over my hand as I whisper her name
into the darkness.

Chapter 15

Laney

Work has been a bitch this week. Any holiday always brings crowds but the two weeks leading up to Christmas are always crazy. Kids are out of school and they end up running around and screaming, trying to touch all the fish, and not listening to their frazzled parents. Today has been exactly that but on a continuous loop.

I reach for my bottle of wine and sigh. I need a few days off but I know the people that have families need their time off more than I do. Someday I will have a family to rush home to. Until then, I will agonize over wanting a cat and worrying I will become the lonely cat lady.

The knock on my door makes me jump. I set my wine down and look out the window. I recognize Max's car right away.

Pulling open the door, I laugh. He holds an envelope out for me with a huge grin on his face. "What's this?"

"Therapy." He shrugs his shoulders. "I promised I'd drop it off. I'm off to the studio."

He hugs me and then runs back out to his car. I wave as he pulls away and then focus my attention back on the letter in my hands. I have no idea what it is but I'm excited to find out. I tear into it, not caring about ruining the envelope. My breath catches when I start to read.

Dear   Laney,
I hope this doesn't come off as corny but the therapists

all feel that writing down our feelings is the best way to start to heal. I think they have it in for me because they know I write lyrics. The past few weeks have been really good for me. It's been the hardest thing I've ever done in my life but I have been without a drink for nearly four weeks. I've extended my stay by a few weeks to make sure I'm ready to start the next part of my life. I miss everyone but this is for me and I've decided it's ok to be selfish right now.

When Dell died, she took a part of my soul with her. I know that's no surprise to anyone but sometimes saying it out loud makes it more real. She was the first person in the world that I truly loved. She was my first everything. It's still hard to imagine walking through the world without her. I've been so full of darkness and sorrow. I was angry that the world went on for everyone else while I felt like mine had ended. The last eight months have been a complete blur, except for one important thing. You.

Lane, you became a light in the darkness for me. I don't know when it happened. Maybe right away. I'm not sure I'll ever know exactly. I just know that your friendship saved me. I wanted to end my life so many times and somehow, you were always there to show me that there was still some hope. You accepted my fucked up mess and didn't try to clean it up. You just stood by my side while I aimlessly tried to find some purpose and you let me make mistakes. Everyone else either enabled it or tried to fix me. Not you. You saw into my darkness and held my hand while I figured it out myself. The words thank you will never be enough.

A few weeks ago, I turned to you to numb my pain. You never questioned it and gave me everything I needed. You were completely selfless and it has caused me so much guilt. I don't ever want you to feel used. Making love to you was not just something that helped me forget. It was something that helped me heal. I'd never shared that with anyone else and sharing it with you was far more than I ever expected. You were kind and gentle, forgiving and selfless, and more than anything, loving. Being with you was easy and I felt so much guilt for not feeling bad about it at the time. Being here, I've realized that it wasn't just physical for me. I started to feel something for you and I know that isn't fair to you. One of the steps we have to work through requires that we don't get involved with anyone. I find this one bullshit but I understand it.

Lane, you mean the world to me. Your friendship is shelter in the storm. I've screwed up so many things in my life and I refuse to let our friendship be one of them. I cannot allow this to be a rebound because you mean far too much to me. I can't get lost in the physical to help heal the emotional. You deserve someone who will be able to love you openly and freely. You deserve a man that isn't in the spotlight and stalked and chased. You deserve someone who can take you out to dinner without cameras and someone who will be home every night to hold you. You deserve someone without so much baggage. I'm not sure there is someone perfect enough for you but I will damn sure help you find him if he's out there.

This letter is me telling you the truth. I love Della. She was supposed to be my once in a lifetime. Being here, away from all the stresses, has allowed me to picture a twice in a lifetime. It's helped me realize that I gave her the majority of my youth and early adulthood and I gave her the best years I've had so far. But, I also know that I have a lot of years ahead of me to share with someone. It will be a long time before I can give someone my heart completely. I'd be honored to have someone just like you. They say time heals all wounds. I'm starting to believe that. But I fear time may also be my enemy. The time I need to heal will probably be longer than anyone has to wait. I have feelings for you that I can't explain. In time, I will work through them. For now, I'm asking you not to wait. You deserve better than that. Don't let someone that could be amazing pass you by while you wait for someone who isn't even sure he can open his heart completely again.

It may be presumptuous to even say these things to you. Looking into your eyes the last time we were together made me realize I may not be alone in these feelings. If I am, I have now completely embarrassed myself. I want you to know that the time we shared was more special than I ever imagined it would be. You are an amazing woman, Adelaine Jones, and I am honored to have shared a little part of your life. I hope when I come home, your friendship will continue to be there to light my way. My life is not nearly as dark as it has been but I will still need a safe haven

*when the storm rolls in.
Love, Griff*

I stare at the letter for a few more minutes. Tears roll down my cheeks. I want to run to him and tell him everything will be ok. He's just as conflicted as I am. The only difference is that I am ready to open my heart up completely and he's a long way from that. I know he is letting me go so I can find someone who is available to love me. I'm just not sure I want to do that. Somewhere along the line, I started to have some feelings for him. I don't know what they are and I'm not sure I ever will.

When my text alert sounds, I put the letter into the top drawer of my desk and take a deep breath. I will give him all the time he needs. If he's ready someday and I haven't found the right person, I'd be honored to be at his side.

I grab my phone and check the message.

Double non date tonight? Rach, Max and I are heading out to Bilkas for dinner at seven. Join us?

I can't help but smile. Chance doesn't give up, despite how many times I tell him it will never happen. His non date invitations are always interesting but the idea of hanging out with them tonight is exactly what I need. Being with them always makes me feel closer to Harley.

Ok. See you at seven.

Bilkas is a quiet little restaurant on the outskirts of the city. It's always full and the food is amazing. The owners moved here from the East Coast and their down home cooking always brings a smile to my face. I guarantee I will eat way too much and leave with a stomach ache but I can't help myself.

Rachel walks in right behind me. She's become a good friend through this tragedy and I know the help she's given the band is invaluable. Max is hot on her heels and I laugh when I see his lovesick eyes. I've decided denial is his middle name but who am I to judge?

"Hey, Lane." He pulls me into a hug. "Do any light reading lately?"

I slap him on the chest and he laughs. "It was a nice letter. Thanks for delivering it to me."

"Hey, beautiful." Chance pulls me into a hug. "Thanks for coming out."

"How could I say no? Two of my favorite men in one place. I'd be crazy to say no." I smile at him and his face lights up. Charm seems to just ooze from him. If my heart weren't already somewhere else, it would be easy to fall for it.

He takes my hand and leads me to our reserved table. After pulling out my chair, he waits for me to sit before he helps me push it back in. He winks at Rachel and Max just shakes his head. A playboy at heart and it makes me laugh. The day he falls for someone, I am going to applaud her for taming the beast that is Lennon Chancellor.

After we order, we swap stories of Christmas breaks growing up and of our favorite presents. It's hard to believe that it's almost that time of year again. Unlike the rest of the guys, Chance seems to have good memories of his childhood. Someday I will ask him how he ended up with Liquid Regret. For now, I will sit back and enjoy the company of the people that are like family to me.

Max's phone rings and without looking, he answers it. "Max Callum."

His face goes white and he looks at the number on the caller ID. He looks around the restaurant, his eyes sweeping the faces of all the other patrons. When he seems satisfied that he isn't being watched, he cuts off whoever is talking on the other line.

"I don't know how you got this number." His voice is a strained whisper. "Don't call me again or my lawyer will be in touch."

I squint my eyes and tilt my head. He makes eye contact with me and gives me the slightest shake of his head. I won't pry but whoever it is has him scared.

"I don't care about your money. I don't need it anymore." He ends the call, slams his phone down on the table and excuses himself.

The three of us sit in stunned silence as we watch him disappear out the front door of Bilkas. I want to go after him but Rachel is standing up before I can even move. Chance reaches over and grabs his phone. He looks at his call log.

"Benjamin Maxwell." He looks at me. "Isn't he a senator or something?"

The memory of Morgan talking to Max runs through my mind. She called him Maxwell. At first I just thought she was crazy. Now I can't help wondering if Max is hiding something and the name Maxwell isn't just a mistake.

"Why would Senator Maxwell be offering Max money?" Chance waves the waitress over and asks her to box up all the food to go. "I think we should go check on him."

I put my hand on his arm. "I'll go. Meet me outside when you have the food." Seeing Chance worry about Max touches a soft spot in my heart.

I can't help but think of Harley. It's not like I do that a thousand times a day or anything. I know there's more to the story and that Harley knows what it is. I hope that whatever this secret is isn't something that can

tear everyone apart. I'm not sure the
guys could handle much more.

Chapter 16

OSHUA

I'm so afraid I'm going to take one look at this piece of shit and want to smash through the Plexiglas that is supposed to protect me from him. What a joke. He's the lucky one here. If I could reach through this phone and rip his throat out, I'd do it. I'd risk the rest of my life to get revenge for what he did to my family. There are no second chances in my book. Jail is too good for this bastard.

His smug look makes me want to commit murder. I need to control myself. I pride myself on being completely unaffected by everything around me. This is no different. My look of indifference will get him talking. He's got nothing to gain from being silent.

"Joshua Seymour. Never thought I'd see you again." His smile makes me furious.

"You won't again. Just coming to get some answers from you, Lex. When I walk out of here, you'll never have to see me again." He has no fucking clue.

"How's golden boy, Harley? Drink himself to death yet?" Lex laughs.

"Matter of fact, he's sober. Everyone is heading to Max's for Christmas dinner. Shame you can't join us this year." I pick a piece of lint off my jacket. He will not know my hatred. Not yet.

"Why are you here?" Aha. He's angry. I can use this to my advantage.

"I stopped by to wish you a Merry Christmas, Lex. I have a little something for you but you'll get it later. For now, I want to know why. I understand why Oksana did it. The sick bitch couldn't even see Harley wouldn't want her if she was the last woman on Earth. But you. You I don't understand. You let her control you like a little bitch. You were the strongest man I knew but you let some overpriced whore convince you to do her bidding. Unbelievable."

I know the second I have him. His eyes darken and squint. The smile turns to a scowl. It's like taking candy from a baby.

"She's not a whore. And it sure as fuck wasn't her idea. She hesitated. She tried to stop me. No one stops me when I've made up my mind. She's mine and I would have done anything to make her happy." Lex is yelling into the phone. Drops of spit hit the Plexiglas as he screams. "I've loved Oksana forever. Not my fault she loved Harley. I kept sitting back waiting for him to fuck up. All those women out on the road, throwing themselves at him. It was only a matter of time. But that piece of shit never took the bait. Oksana wanted him and the only way to give her what she wanted was to take Della away from him."

Unfuckingbelievable. "You did this because you fell in love with the whore?"

He slams his hand against the glass. "Don't you dare talk about her that way. Fuck you, Seymour! All Harley had to do was fuck up once. Once! Della would have left him so fast and Oksana would have had what she always wanted. I saw the way he looked at Mia's friend. I tried to tell Dell that he was going to cheat. She knew he wouldn't be unfaithful. She trusted him. Even through all the threats. She kept believing the best in him. All she kept saying was that Laney would be good for him if something happened to her."

"Della trusted you, you piece of shit." I'm done acting unaffected. I can feel my face burning. "You were her family."

His laugh stuns me. "She had it coming. She let both of us in like we weren't a threat at all. She was standing there in the kitchen cutting up a lime and I asked her to hand me the knife. Stupid bitch handed it right to me. Didn't even scream. Just kept asking me why. It was beautiful.

Watching someone taking their last breath. You should have seen it."

I've had enough. I slam the phone down and stand up. He just laughs at me. I nod at the guard without hesitation. "Merry Christmas, Lex."

Chapter 17

I'm sitting in my car in Max's driveway, eyes closed, listening to the sound of the waves crashing against the shore. My doctors thought I wasn't ready to leave but I needed to be with my family today. I suppose it helps that Della wasn't a big fan of Christmas and we didn't exchange gifts or celebrate much. This year, I want to spend the day with laughter and presents and celebrating the things that I've missed over the last month and a half. I have my sponsor on speed dial and Rachel on standby.

When I heard everyone was getting together at Max's for an early dinner, I knew I had to be here. No one knows I'm home except for

Joshua. He picked me up last night and grilled me most of the trip home. I'm aware I fucked up. I'm also aware of how worried he is, and not just about the image of the band, but about my well-being.

I walk to the door and it's like I'm seeing everything for the first time. The air is cool and the sun is starting to set. It's quiet and as I take a deep breath, I smile. I've been in such a fog for so long and I've missed so much. It's a long road ahead but I'm ready to travel it.

I don't even knock. The front door is unlocked and I push my way in. I hear laughter from the back deck and it fills an empty part of my heart. When I step outside, I imagine the reaction will be a mixture of joy and guilt. They will all try to hide their wine or whatever they're drinking and look at me with pity. I'm used to that reaction. Every time I tried to quit drinking, I'd get that same response if I showed up somewhere unannounced.

I slide the door open and all conversation stops. Instead of pity, they're all smiling and laughing. Mia and Rachel both run at the door and throw their arms around me. Damien is right behind them, arms open wide and a smile as big as I've ever seen. Max winks at me from his seat at the side of the pool. Chance approaches slowly, uncertainty written all over his face. He waits for me to respond and I pull him into me.

"Thank you, brother." I hug him. His brutal honesty is what made me finally see the light. "You saved me."

"No." He pats my back. "You saved you. I just helped you see you were worth it."

When I turn back to the table, Laney is smiling. Christ, she's a site for sore eyes. Her hair is pulled up into a loose ponytail. Her cream colored sweater hugs her curves and I have an overwhelming urge to take her into my arms. It isn't just a lust response. My heart hammers in my chest and I can't help the huge grin that spreads across my face.

"Come here, woman." She giggles as I pull her against my chest. The smell of her shampoo is too addictive and I can't stop myself from burying my nose in her neck and letting out a quiet moan. When she stiffens in my arms, I whisper against her ear. "I missed you, Lane."

Her whisper is beyond sexy. "I missed you, too."

Chance walks up behind us and clears his throat. "I've been working on this for weeks. Weeks! I still haven't gotten that kind of reaction. You can thank me for warming her up for you."

Laney pulls away from me and slaps him in the chest. His laugh is contagious and as he starts to run, she throws her arms out and shoves him. As he starts his freefall into the pool, he snags her wrists and pulls her in right behind him. Her scream as she hits the cold water makes me laugh. Chance starts splashing her as soon as she breaks the surface. She's trying to be angry but the corners of her mouth twitch as she fights her smile.

I can't help my eyes from roaming and when I see how

transparent her sweater is soaking wet, I have a huge urge to growl at everyone. I need to get her out of the water and into something dry, and dark, and that covers her completely. I wonder if Max has a turtle-neck I could put on her. I extend my hand to help her out and just before her fingers touch mine, Chance grabs my wrist and pulls me in, surprising the shit out of me.

As I surface, Laney is yelling. "What are you, six?"

Chance doesn't even miss a beat. "Probably more like seven and a half or eight. I have a tape measure if you want to measure it. It's not a party until someone gets a ruler out."

"Max, go get it. I'd like to beat him with it." Laney shivers as she pulls herself from the pool.

"Yeah, baby. Now we're talking." Chance is hot on her heels and she starts laughing.

She reaches between his legs and he jumps in surprise. Her eyes squint like she's concentrating. I know I should be jealous but I see that gorgeous brain of hers working. "Seems like all you do is talk. Cancel that ruler, Max. Would be a waste to pull it out for all two inches."

"Shrinkage, Lane. I was in the pool." When she starts to walk away, Chance is at a loss. "It's cold."

Before she opens the door to walk inside, she turns and looks him right in the eyes. "A better comeback would have been something like 'that's just the tip'. You're slipping, Chance."

"I think I love that woman." Chance starts laughing and I have the sudden urge to swing.

"Get in line, Bud." Max helps me out of the pool. "There are towels in the warmer in my bathroom. Help yourself to anything in my closet. Anything, Griff."

I can't help but chuckle on my way to his room. Some of my things are still here, probably all over the guest room floor since I was hardly able to take a shower, let alone pick up anything. I'm not sure if he's sparing me the frustration of seeing what I'd done to my room or if it was code for something. Either way, I'm heading to his closet.

When I turn the corner to his closet, I stop dead in my tracks. Laney is standing there, dripping, and reaching for a sweatshirt on a higher shelf. Before I can offer her help, I take in her beauty. Her hair is matted against her cheeks. Her sweater is like a second skin, soaked against her like it was made just for her. She's gorgeous.

I reach over her and pull the sweatshirt down. I smile at her when she takes it. "Thanks." Her body shivers.

It's just instinct to touch her. I can't help myself. I rub my hands up and down her arms. She snuggles against my chest. Water drips onto the carpet but I don't give a shit. She's in my arms and in this moment, that is all that matters.

After a few minutes, I can hear everyone coming back into the house. I know our moment is over but I'm thankful for the time I did get, even if we were standing alone in Max's closet.

She smiles up at me and I want to fall at her feet and apologize for everything I've put her through the past few months. I want to tell her to run away from me as fast as she can. I want to push her away and tell her that there's someone out there so much better for her. But, the selfish part of me stays silent and stares back at her. My whole life stopped, everything went numb, every part of me died when Damien walked through my hotel room door. This many months later, I realize that the only time I can breathe is when she's standing with me. The only time I feel my heart beat is when I'm looking at her. This can't just be a rebound, can it?

"We should probably get back out there." Laney shivers and I know I should leave her alone to change. I'm just not ready to go yet.

"Let me help you." I pull her sweater off without waiting for permission. Dropping it to the floor, I don't take my eyes off of her. Her skin breaks out in goosebumps. "I missed you so much, Lane."

She stands perfectly still, allowing my eyes to roam over her entire body. I reach behind her and unhook her bra. She lets it fall to the floor and doesn't try to cover up. She's magnificent. I want to slam the closet door and pin her against it. I want to pin her to the ground and make love to her until she can't move. Instead, I will be a gentleman and help her get dressed. I've been home a couple hours and I can't expect her to just jump into my arms like I never left.

I help her into Max sweatshirt that looks more like a dress on her than a shirt. She takes her wet pants off and sighs. "I have no idea what I'm going to put on." Her laugh makes me smile.

"Give me a few minutes. Max may be a good boy, but he's no saint. Let me see if I can find something that one of the women left behind." When she scrunches up her nose, I chuckle. "You're right. That's probably a long shot."

"Laney? Are you in here?" Max clears his throat. "I have some yoga pants of Rachel's if you need them."

I belly laugh as Laney's jaw drops. She mouths "Rachel?" to me as she sticks her head out of the closet. "Max Callum to the rescue."

Max winks at her as she takes them from his hands. "I will always be your knight in shining armor." When he sees my face, he starts laughing. "Shit. I forgot. That's Chance's job."

"Thank you, Max." She stands on her tip toes and gives him a kiss on the cheek. Bastard.

I grab the closet door and start to close it on him. "Yes, thank you, Max." As the door clicks shut, I hear him laughing.

"Cave-men." Laney smiles at me while she pulls on Rachel's yoga pants. "It's good to have you home, you tease."

I stand there staring like an idiot as she leaves the room. Admitting that I want her scares the shit out of me. But, I can't deny it anymore. I want her.

Chapter 18

I feel like I'm back in high school. The butterflies are beating the shit out of my stomach. Every time I look at him, he's looking at me and I have to look away. The only difference is that in high school, I'd be giggling and this would be a crush. I'm not sure it's that innocent. I know his letter said he wanted to me to be happy with someone and not waste my time on waiting but I don't want to. If my heart is in charge, I'll wait. If my head it in charge, I'll wait.

The way he looks at me isn't like a man that wants me to find someone else. He looks at me like he's hungry and I'm his next meal. He looks like a man that wants to take his time worshipping me. He looks at me like a man who wants me on my knees in front of him. He does not look at me like a man who wants to walk away.

"Found this under the tree." Mia winks at me.

I look around the room and everyone is chatting. The only person paying any attention to me is Harley. He smiles at me and the butterflies start again. My hands shake as I unwrap the shiny package. The small turquoise box makes my heart pound. A gift from Tiffany's is intimate and means something. I'm afraid to open it.

My eyes lock with Harley's and he laughs. He nods at the box in my hands and I giggle. I want to stand up and scream, "Harley got me a present!" But that's sure to scare him off, so I'll play it cool. I can do this. Deep breath.

I lift the lid and I almost stop breathing. Inside, a beautiful necklace sparkles back at me. The delicate silver chain holds a small sun pendant. I run my finger over it and smile. It's simple and beautiful and absolutely perfect. The words of his letter make perfect sense. The light in his darkness, the shelter from his storm. I've never received a gift more meaningful.

I'm so mesmerized that I don't hear Harley approaching. He takes the box from me and whispers, "let me help you."

I swallow the lump in my throat and hold my hair out of the way. When it touches my neck, I can't help but touch it. Tears form in my eyes. "It's so pretty. Thank you, Griff."

He kisses my neck, then whispers in my ear. "You are my sunshine, Lane."

He sits behind me, his legs on either side of me, filling me with an emotion that is completely foreign to me. I lean into him as if the others in the room don't exist. I know Max knows something is going on but the rest of them have no idea. Mia will kill me if she finds out this way. But in this moment, on Christmas evening, sitting back against Harley, my life feels totally full. He wraps his arms around my waist and puts his chin on my shoulder. I shiver.

"Are you ok with this?" His breath on my neck sends a bolt of excitement to my heart.

I nod and relax into him. My arms cross against his and I sigh. My eyes close for a minute and I send a silent prayer up to Della, thanking her for making him the amazing man he is today. When the room gets quiet, I open one eye. I shouldn't have done that. Everyone is staring. Shit.

Mia is on her feet, eyes wide, mouth open in shock. Damien is sitting on the couch shaking his head with a smirk on his face. I know that he suspected my feelings, but I doubt he ever thought Harley felt anything. Joshua is stoic as always but the person I'm most worried about is Chance. I was honest from the very beginning. I told him my heart belonged to someone else but I cringe thinking about how it feels knowing it's one of his best friends. Harley aside, I'd never have had a fling with Chance. He's fun and gorgeous but he collects women like some people collect baseball cards. I can't just be another number, even if I am in mint condition compared to some of the women I've seen him take home.

"It's about fucking time you two came out of my closet." Max laughs at himself and I roll my eyes.

"We weren't hiding. We're just taking things one minute at a time. Right now is a good minute." Harley smiles at me and I swear I melt. I'm a useless puddle of lust.

Mia covers her mouth with her hand and she starts to cry. Damien is on his feet right away as she sobs. He looks worried but Mia pushes him away. "Harley is smiling."

She runs at us and hugs us both. "I'm so happy to see you smiling."

Harley laughs. "I've got a long way to go, Mia. I'm still a fucked up mess. Lane and I need to have a long talk, but I hope she'll give me a chance."

I turn to face him. "You don't even have to ask that, Griff. I'll give you a million chances. And if you need another one, I'll give you that one too."

When our lips touch, the rest of the world fades away. It's soft and gentle and lasts only a second but it's enough to tell me what I need to know. He's ready to take his first step forward.

"Come on, Romeo." Chance holds the back door open. "Give me a hand with the grill."

I can't help but watch Harley walk away. Max's sweatpants are way too long on him and seeing him in the oversized sweatshirt is totally sexy. I'm so used to seeing him in jeans and a tight t-shirt but he's gorgeous in everything. And out of everything. I giggle to myself. I'm a goner.

"You bitch." Mia slaps my arm and I laugh. "Why didn't you tell me?"

"There was nothing to tell. It's going to be a long road but I'm willing to take it as slowly as he needs to." It's like he has radar and knows I'm talking about him. He turns and looks at me through the glass door. I can tell he's playing with his tongue ring and I can't wait to do the same. "He's broken, Mia. I just want to help pick up the pieces."

I glance around the room again. Rachel is texting and biting her lip. When Max's phone vibrates, he looks at it and gives her the quickest glance before texting back. Speaking of secrets. My laugh makes him look at me and I raise one eye-brow. He just flips me off and keeps texting. Joshua is fidgeting and checking his watch. He probably doesn't want to be here. He doesn't seem too festive and I would bet that the holidays aren't really his thing. He jumps when his phone buzzes and his face completely changes when he reads the text.

"Let's celebrate. It's Christmas. Max, pop that sparkling grape juice I brought." Joshua claps his hands once and laughs. "That sounds so lame."

While Max gets up, I stare back out the window. Chance and Harley are laughing together and I can't help but smile. He looks relaxed and almost happy. The dark circles under his eyes are still there but they're fading. He's still chewing gum like crazy but that just shows me that he's trying so hard to stay sober. I couldn't be more proud of him.

His phone rings and he looks at the screen in confusion. He holds up a finger to Chance and takes a few steps toward the pool. When he freezes, I'm on my feet. His body language changes. I'm not the only one that notices. I see Chance take a few steps toward him and stop.

I can't hear them but when Harley puts his phone back in his pocket, there's a look on his face that I can't place. Chance looks stunned and I can't stop myself from heading for the door. Before I can get there, Chance opens it and steps inside with a confused Harley.

"Are you ok?" My question gets everyone's attention.

"Yeah." He looks right at Damien. "Lex is dead."

Chapter 19

Holy shit. I can't believe I just said those words out loud. A little wave of sadness crashes over me before absolute joy. That motherfucker got everything that was coming to him. The officer told me he'd been stabbed during an altercation with a guard. I didn't have any questions. I don't care where the knife came from or who had it. All I know is that one stab wasn't enough. About thirty more would have been justice. I'll never understand why he did this to me and Della. I'm not sure I want to.

"What?" Damien's voice is quiet.

"I don't know. I just got a call from one of the officers that was investigating Della's death. He said Lex was stabbed to death." Is that my voice? Why does it sound so happy? I'm a sick bastard. I should feel guilty for feeling this way.

Damien pulls me into a hug. "Are you ok?"

"I am. Is that ok? Should I feel bad?"

"Fuck no. He got what he deserved. I just wish we knew why he did it." Max puts his hand on my shoulder.

Joshua pulls me aside. "Can we talk in private?"

I follow him without saying a word. If this is going to be a media circus or another fucking press conference, I'm going to have to kick his ass. I know he's only doing his job but I'm not putting my face back out in front of the paparazzi so soon after getting home from a month in rehab.

"I saw Lex and I asked him why he did what he did. If you're ever ready to know, I'll tell you. He mentioned your loyalty to Della and the faith she had in you. When all the threats started coming in, she talked with him about them. I thought you should know that she talked about you moving on if something ever happened to her."

"I can't do this, Joshua. Not now. It's too soon to face anything else." He puts his hand on my shoulder and I know he understands.

"Fair enough. But she thought Laney would be good for you." He takes a step away before he adds something that floors me. "For the record, I do too. I want you to be happy, Griff. Not just for the band, but for you. It's time."

My hands are shaking as I take a seat in Max's foyer. This time, it isn't because I need a drink. Although the thought of alcohol has been in the forefront of my mind all day, I refuse to give in to the darkness anymore. I won't let Della down again. I won't let myself down anymore. I won't let the light that Laney has added to my life be dragged through the nothingness that encompassed my whole life not so long ago. Tonight my hands shake out of fear. A fear of moving on and forgetting what I had. A fear of letting go of something so precious to move on to something else that is different but not any less life changing.

It's hard for me to grasp any conversation where Della imagined a world without her in it. She was the most selfless woman in the world and knowing that, she would want me to find happiness and start living again. Hearing it from Joshua only validates everything I already knew.

"Hey." Max takes a seat next to me on the floor of the entryway. "I know you probably need a minute but I heard what Joshua said about Della. I want to tell you something."

I don't need to say anything. Max's zest for life makes him someone that won't let anything go unsaid. Even if I pleaded with him to give me some time, he wouldn't leave until he said what he needed to. He's always been this way. It's part of the reason he loved Della. I know he must have seen a lot of himself in her. They were so much alike. I need to take comfort in that.

"When Dell got that first threat at work, she called me to make sure you were ok. She'd been so worried about you, even though she was the one that had gotten the note. She made me promise her that I'd watch over you if anything ever happened to her. I told her we'd keep her safe and she was so stubborn that she made me promise her anyway."

When he takes a huge breath, I know that whatever's coming next is going to hurt. "When she left that last time, she made me promise again. But not just that. She made me promise to keep you sober. I failed her on that but I was too destroyed to even keep my promise."

"Max." My voice shakes.

He holds up his hand and continues. "She told me that she knew you were in good hands with us and that she'd spend every second she could looking down on us. She said that Laney would be the person she'd pick for you if she had any say in it. It was like a part of her knew what she was going home to. She was saying goodbye and I didn't even realize it. I watched Lex get in the limo behind her and I just went on with my day. I got on that fucking tour bus and just knew she'd be there when we all got home."

I can't say anything. Max is falling apart right in front of me and there's nothing I can do to help him. I need air. I can't breathe. If Della was saying goodbye, she didn't realize it. She couldn't have or I would have known it. I would have stopped it. She was always so brave. We talked a million times a day and she was never worried about anything but me.

I walk to the back door and practically rip it from the hinges. I don't say a word to anyone. I can't. I take the stairs to the beach two at a time. I need to breathe.

I let the sand squish between my toes. It's cold and it makes me shiver. The waves roll in as a reminder that life goes on. I take a deep breath.

"You said goodbye to Max and Lex. Did I just miss it? Did you know, Dell?" I look at the sky and watch as the moon breaks through the clouds. "I miss you so much."

When the wind picks up, I laugh. She's always with me. I close my eyes and let the breeze hit me. It's warm for this time of year and I know it's her. She may be gone from this Earth but she's still in my heart and I will keep her safe there.

I hear footsteps on the stairs behind me. I know it's her before she speaks. There's an electricity when Laney is near me that can't be denied. It's always been there. Even as early as our first flight together. She radiates confidence and that draws me to her. Now I know that Della felt it too. There's so much comfort in that.

I turn and pull her to me. I need her in my arms. She nuzzles my chest and I'm a fucking goner. I need this woman in my life. I tilt her chin up and press my lips against hers. She moans into my mouth and I'm instantly hard. The sounds she makes drive me insane. Her tongue runs over my piercing and it's my turn to moan. Her mouth is magic, her tongue is heaven.

"I told myself I'd take this slow." I pull away and hug her. "You make it impossible to not want to rip your clothes off."

She laughs. "All good things are worth waiting for."

I hold her against me for a few minutes while we watch the waves. The night is clear and the moon is bright. I feel her breathing in time with me and know our hearts are in sync too. I run my fingers through her soft hair and her arms wrap tighter around my waist. She smells good, her skin is warm and soft and I want to feel her against me.

"We've been out here about ten minutes. Do you think that's long enough?" When she looks at me confused, I kiss the tip of her nose. "Do you think we waited long enough? Because I can't wait to get lost inside you."

"I think it's been way too long." She crashes her lips against mine and as I lift her, her legs wrap around my waist. The kiss is heated and the slow burn starts in my chest. "Fuck me, Harley."

"Not tonight." I rest my forehead against hers and smile. "Tonight, I'm going to make love to you."

I never realized the drive across town took so long. Laney's curled up in the front seat, head on my shoulder, lightly snoring against me. I want to pull the car over and hold her. I feel so emotional that I swear I've become a teenage girl. I feel like I'm a second away from bursting into tears from whatever these feelings are that are coursing through my veins. My chest is on fire, my heart banging out a rhythm against my rib cage, my palms all sweaty. It's been a long time since I've felt this.

I try to think back and remember the moment I realized I was falling for Della. I don't even remember a life before her. The second I met her, I knew she was the one. I remember the burn in my chest and the constant pounding of my heart. I don't remember the clammy hands or the bipolar feeling that any second I could cry. Rachel is going to have a field day during our session tomorrow.

Do I love Laney? I don't know. I certainly feel a hell of a lot more than like for her. The first night I met her, in that smoky bar, she threatened to lick me. *'If I lick him, he's mine'*. The memory makes me smile. Chance hadn't even given me a second to respond before announcing I had a wife and that she should take a chance on him, pun intended. She's the first woman I ever looked at a second time. I thought nothing of it at the time. When she challenged my stamina on the plane on the way to our concert, I'd felt a knot form in my stomach.

I never would have cheated on Dell. No chance in hell. She was my first love and always will be. Looking back at all our interactions, I see why she thought Laney would be a good match for me if something ever happened to her. Where Dell was beautiful and subtle and calm, Laney was loud, outspoken and hot. She challenged me immediately and I responded to her feisty sass by fighting back. She challenges Chance in the same way and even though it's all about the game, I want to make sure I stake my claim before he has a chance to.

Laney stirs against me and I put my hand on her thigh. She moans in her sleep. We're only a few miles from her apartment. I know I said I'd take my time with her tonight. Truth be told, I'm not sure I can. Just the sight of her curled against me has me rock hard. Hearing her moan makes me want to bury myself so deeply that she screams my name before I pound into her tight body.

I run my hand further up her thigh. Even in her sleep, she responds to me. My fingers brush against the apex of her thighs. She arches into my hand and whimpers. These fucking yoga pants need to go. I can feel her heat and I'm coming undone.

My tires squeal as I pull into her parking space. It's pitch black and exactly what I need. We aren't making it out of this car until she comes.

Chapter 20

I'm having the most amazing dream. Harley's here with me, touching me where I need him most. I can feel his fingers and his mouth. My body is on fire. Consciousness stirs just on the outskirts of my mind and I force my eyes to stay closed. I've never had a dream like this.

My hands tangle in his hair, pulling his mouth against me, grinding against his tongue. Fuck, this feels so good. He hums against me and then circles his tongue against my clit over and over and over. I can hear myself begging, pleading to let me come. I'm so horny and I need the relief.

My fingers run over my sweatshirt but his hands stop me. I

can feel his fingers under my shirt, rubbing against my breasts. My nipples harden and he shoves the cup of my bra down and pulls my nipple ring. My toes curl and my head falls back in silent worship.

I'm so close and my eyes start to flicker open. No no no! I want to stay asleep. I need to finish. I try to stretch but I'm stuck. Panic starts to hit me. I'm in Harley's car, asleep on his shoulder and I don't know how long I've been asleep or how much I've said out loud.

I keep my eyes closed, trying to compose myself. The onslaught of pleasure doesn't stop. I feel a massive orgasm starting to build. My legs start to shake and he moans.

Wait. I try to shake myself all the way awake. My eyes snap open and Harley is leaning over me, licking, sucking, fucking me with his mouth. I look out the window and realize we're in my parking lot. When he pulls my nipple ring for the second time, I'm done.

My back arches off the car seat and my legs clamp down around his head. I come so hard that I swear I've flooded the front seat. "Oh God. Oh God."

"Fuck." Harley licks me clean and I'm so close to exploding again. "I've never tasted anything like you. So sweet. I'll never get enough."

I'm covered in sweat, pants around my ankles, breathing out of control. I'm boneless and completely at his mercy.

"I need you." He slams his car door and runs around to open mine.

I'm in slow motion, basking in my post orgasmic glow.

That's not fast enough for him. He pulls me out of the car and carries me to the front door. My hands shake as I try to unlock it. He just keeps taking deep breaths, patiently waiting for me to open it. When the latch gives way, he pushes us inside, kicking the door shut with his foot. He doesn't stop until we get to the bedroom. I giggle at the concentration on his face. He's fucking gorgeous.

He throws me onto the bed and the air leaves my lungs in an unattractive oomph. He starts laughing and I can't help but do the same. He takes his sweatshirt off at a snail's pace. When he pulls it over his head, his eyes meet mine. He winks and bites his lip. He swings it around over his head and throws it toward the closet. He circles his hips as he unties his sweats and I'm trying so hard not to laugh. I'm not sure if he's trying to be sexy or make me smile but it's the funniest thing I've ever seen.

Harley flings one shoe toward the closet and trips over the pants wrapped around his ankles. I throw my head back and laugh so hard, my eyes fill with tears. He pokes his lip out at me and I laugh even harder. I can't help myself. I've never seen him so happy.

He crawls onto the bed, covering my body with his. He makes it to my waist before he loses his balance again and falls on top of me. His laugh is the most beautiful sound I've ever heard. We both struggle to catch our breath. He rests his head against my stomach and lets out months of frustration through laughter. I've never felt closer to him. It's clumsy and it's the most romantic thing in the world to me.

"You're my joy after sorrow, my laughter after all my tears, my proof that there's life after death." His mouth meets mine in a gentle kiss. "You saved me, Lane. You made me believe in living again."

I roll him onto his back and get lost in his kiss. His mouth is warm and soft and in total contradiction to the hard muscles of his body. I swallow his moan as I drag my finger down his abs. They ripple under my touch and I need to kiss every inch of him. I lick his nipples that are so beautifully pierced. I run my tongue over the snake tattooed around his right shoulder. I trace the dice tattooed on his left wrist. Every inch of him is beautiful. I place a kiss on the heart tattooed in the middle of his chest. His body is mine and someday, I hope to have his heart.

I center myself over him and slide onto his waiting cock. He moans as I wrap around him. His eyes never leave mine as I begin to rock against him. Every stroke rubs just the right spot. I bite my lip to keep from losing control. He reaches forward and takes my hands. Looking down, he kisses the inside of each wrist. It's so intimate and I fall just a little harder for him.

I lean forward and lie against his chest. I roll my hips and my clit is met with the friction of his pelvic bone. I need more. My pace quickens and before long, I'm panting against him. That familiar tingle that only Harley gives me starts in my toes. I turn my head and bite his nipple, playing with the barbell through it. He bucks against me and I know I've found his weakness. I do it again and again. Each time, he growls and slams into me.

"Keep it up. This won't last another minute." He pulls my hair and buries his tongue in my mouth.

I pull away and sit up. I pick up my pace, each stroke of his erection hitting the G-spot that Harley finds so easily. "I've never felt this good with anyone."

His smile melts my heart. His eyes wrinkle in the corner and sparkle back at me. I reach out and trace his eye-brows, his cheeks, and then his lips. The stubble on his chin is such a turn on. I prefer him scruffy. I prefer him quiet and happy. In this moment, I'm not with Harley the rock god.

Tonight, I'm making love to Griffin Miles and it's the most amazing feeling in the world.

My orgasm starts slowly and I lean my head back in ecstasy. It's a slow burn and I ride out every second of pleasure. My body tightens around him and his forehead wrinkles in concentration. I can feel my orgasm dripping from my body onto his. He takes a deep breath, pushing away his impending climax.

He grunts and his eyes flutter closed. "Shit. I'm so close."

I smile as I grind harder. The moment he comes is the most amazing feeling in the world. I concentrate on making him lose all control. I need to feel him, hot and wild, filling me with everything he has.

He reaches forward and pinches my clit hard. The pain gives way to extreme pleasure and I start to come without warning. I scream so loud that it echoes around the room. My climax rushes out of me and soaks him. He runs his fingers through it and brings them to his mouth. The look on his face alone could make me come again. He sucks his fingers clean and reaches for more. He moans long and low as he licks them clean again.

"I'm going to come." He bucks wildly under me and I feel him swell. He arches off the bed as his body spasms and hot liquid hits me, coating my walls, making me want more. "Fuck, Lane."

His mouth crashes against me. His kiss is hungry and I feel like he's eating me alive. He sucks on my tongue and growls when I whimper.

He holds my head so I couldn't get away even if I wanted to. I get lost in his kiss until I feel his fingers circling my soaked clit. It's so sensitive and I want to tell him to stop but my body wants to come again.

"There aren't words to describe how good sex with you is. I just need to show you." His voice is raspy and it's sexy as hell. "I want to feel you come on me again. I want to feel you squeezing my cock with that beautiful pussy. I want to hear you beg for more. And when you're done, and you think you can't take anymore, I want you to ride my face. I want to feel you dripping down my chin. I want to spend the rest of the night licking you clean and making you dirty again."

If words could make me come, I would have. He told me once that my body was made for fucking. I disagree. My body was made to fuck his and his alone. We fit together in every way and I've never been so wet and so needy in all my life. Challenge accepted. I plan on spending all night coming. I plan on returning the favor until there's nothing left inside him. When the sun comes up tomorrow, I want to be so sore that every time I move, I remember where he's been.

His fingers continue their slow rhythm and I feel my body start to shake. Feeling him inside me, filling me and holding completely still while his hands bring me to climax is the most intense feeling. I let go completely, riding his fingers without a care in the world.

As I come apart, he smiles at me. Through my sexual fog, I smile back. As his fingers start again, he looks me right in the eyes. "I could fall for you so easily, Adelaine Jones."

Chapter 21

"Have you thought about drinking today?" Rachel's question is the same one I hear from everyone that counsels me. I've become a big believer in therapy. It's saved me.

"Not as often as I usually do." I think back on the two weeks that Laney and I have spent glued to each other. "The true test starts tomorrow."

"Are you worried the press tour will bring too much temptation?" Here comes that damn pen Rachel loves so much.

"I'm better equipped than I was the last time. I think the desire will be there but I don't need to drink." I take a deep breath. Will there ever be a day I'll be able to look at Rachel and not feel the need to pour my heart out? "Laney will join us the second week. I want her with me the whole time but she insists on working."

Rachel laughs. "How does being away from her make you feel?"

"I'm terrified." It's the truth I've been too scared to admit.

"Why are you terrified?" She puts the pen down. I always know she's serious when the pen goes down.

"I'm scared if I leave, someone will hurt her. I couldn't handle it again. I trust my band. I trust my manager. I trust her. I don't trust anyone else. I trusted Lex and he took away what mattered most. What if he takes her away too?"

"Lex is gone, Griff. He can't hurt you anymore." Rachel's voice is always soothing.

"There's always another Lex out there. Another Oksana. I died the day Della did. The old me did anyway. I'll never be the same." My eyes burn. "My life is so much better than it was six months ago. But I'm different. I won't ever be the man I was a year ago."

"Love heals. I know it's hard to see that on the dark days. You are loved by so many people. There's a lot of good left in the world. I'd hate for you to miss any more of it." She touches my knee and I know she's my friend and not my therapist at the moment.

"I'm not ready to use the love word. I feel it. I'm just afraid to admit it. I think that admitting it is letting go of Della and I'm not sure I can ever do that." I look at Rachel. Her silence speaks volumes. "Laney is amazing. She talks with me about her every day. I can tell her stories and be completely honest and she never judges me. I've never seen even an ounce of jealousy. The woman I loved more than anything is gone and the woman that makes my heart beat helps me keep that love alive. I'm crazy about her, Rach. I'm just scared I'm going to forget about Della."

"Griff, you'll never forget her. She was your entire world for so long. Part of you will always be hers. That doesn't mean another part of you can't belong to someone else. I've gotten a chance to talk to Laney and she really is special. I feel like part of Della stays alive because of the love Laney has for you. You're getting a second chance at love. Some people never even get a first chance."

I refuse to cry anymore. I've spent more than eight months crying and I won't lose any more time feeling sad. Rachel is right. Laney is living proof that I'm a lucky son of a bitch. I can't help but smile. I feel happy and my heart is on the mend.

"Before you go, I want to talk with you about Oksana's trial. I hear they're moving the case to another county because they feel she won't get a fair trial here. What are you feeling?" That fucking pen is back.

"I know what's coming. I know her lawyer will pull some bullshit about how Lex forced her to do it. Maybe he did. I know she'll be found guilty. Part of me wants to see her fry for what she did. But there's this small part of me that hopes she spends the rest of her life in jail and I can get some answers when I'm ready. Joshua talked with me the other night. I know Lex did it because he was in love with Oksana. I know she helped because she was in love with me. Either way, they were both sick. I know what rage feels like. I'm trying to remember that's what she was feeling when she took Della away from me."

Rachel wipes a tear from her cheek. "You've come such a long way. Seven months ago, you wouldn't even talk to me. Now you open your heart and work through your feelings as you talk. The friend in me is so proud of you. The therapist says you won't need to come see me so often anymore."

"What if we fire you?" Her look of confusion makes me realize I may have been too harsh. "You've spent so much time with us as our therapist. It's been hard to be friends without breaking all the patient/ doctor rules you have set up for all of us. There were special circumstances that kept you with us for so long. Maybe it's time to cut you loose and let you settle into our lives in another capacity."

Rachel thinks for a minute and then shakes her head. Her eyes are so sad that I want to hug her. "I don't think I could do that. I've spent so much time developing these relationships with all of you. I enjoy being a part of your lives but I don't know if it could be more than that."

"What if we have a reason for firing you? What if there is greater potential for happiness if you are in our lives in a different way?" If she doesn't catch on in a minute, I'm going to have to spell it out for her. Max + Rachel = forever and all that bullshit.

"I don't know if there would be a good enough reason to break the guidelines that are set."

Before she can say anymore, I cut her off. "I have to disagree. I think there's a guy that stands about six feet three that would fight you on that."

She smiles and her cheeks dip into deep dimples. I'm not sure I've ever seen her smile so wide. "Whatever. Fine. Go pack. Call me if you need me."

"It's been real, Doc, but your services will no longer be needed." I hug her and walk out of her office. I can find another therapist. Max has saved me a million times over. It's time I did him a favor in return.

"I don't want to say goodbye." I bury my face in her hair.

"It's a week. Then I'll meet you on the East Coast and we can be together again. It's a busy time at work and I need to be there to help the other biologists as we bring in the new marine life. I promise you I'll stay safe." She rubs her fingers across my jaw and smiles. "I'm staying with Mia all week. We'll be fine."

"I had Joe check the security system. Everything looks good. He'll be outside every night. Don't let anyone in. Not if you're alone. I mean it, Lane. I don't care if it's Joshua. No one comes in the door if you're alone. Promise me, Lane."

She hugs me. "Griffin, I promise you I'll be careful. You can't live in constant fear that the past is going to repeat itself. Lex is gone and Oksana is locked up with no possibility of getting out. We've been careful in public. It's ok, baby. I promise."

She puts her hand on my chest and I can feel myself relaxing. "I'm sorry. I know I'll be calling you like mad. Just humor me. It's going to take me awhile to trust people again."

There's no judgment in her eyes. "I know. I'll be waiting for your calls. We'll get through this together. You can call me day or night. I'll keep my phone on me the whole week." She stands on her tiptoes and kisses me. "We'll learn to trust the world together. Whatever you need."

The limo pulls in the driveway and I start to panic. Laney sees the change in me and holds my hand. I kiss her lightly before I throw my suitcase in the trunk. I rest my forehead against hers and stare into her mesmerizing blue eyes. A week without seeing her face is way too long. Shit. I'm so screwed. I love this girl.

Max comes slamming out the front door cursing up a storm. He points at me and yells. "You!"

I want to laugh but he's so mad. Laney's eyes widen and I fight like hell to keep the smile off my face. "What?"

"Don't pull the innocent bullshit. You fired Rachel? What the fuck? You think you were the only one she was working with?" He gets right in my face and for a second, I think he might take a swing at me. I brace for impact but he just stands there.

"You're welcome." I laugh and take a step back.

"For what?" His hands ball into fists.

"Now she doesn't work for you anymore. Seems to me that might make things easier." I can see the realization dawn on him the second it happens. "Ah, there it is. Now he gets it."

Laney's laugh echoes through my heart. I hug her before I get into the limo. I wink at her and then point to Joe. He takes his place at her side and she smiles up at him. I'm going to try to relax. I'll call every ten minutes instead of every five.

Max climbs into the back of the limo and stares at me. He won't admit shit to me. That's ok. I'm not blind. I see the way they look at each other. I see the way he watches her when she isn't looking. It's like watching me with Laney. Fear is a powerful thing but if Rachel taught me one valuable lesson, it's to let love heal.

Chapter 22

"This is Cameron, RLTX Wake Up Atlanta. I'm here this morning with the men of Liquid Regret. Welcome back to the Peach State."

Damien takes the lead, like he always does. I'm so thankful that I'm not the face of this band. There's just way too much bullshit to deal with. "Thanks, Cameron. We're happy to be back."

"You started your first tour right here in Atlanta. Rumor has it that you'll be heading back on tour again this summer. Will we see a stop here?"

Joshua is on it and I laugh at his serious tone. "Plans have not been confirmed and the cities and dates are just tentative at this time. We'll release a statement once we have more information."

"This new album is darker than the first one. Can you tell us why?" When Cameron looks at me, I know it's time to face the music, no pun intended.

"My wife was killed 9 months ago. It was a dark time for all of us." I'm surprised at the strength in my voice. I'm overwhelmed by the healing I've done and for the first time, I'm proud of the man I'm becoming in the face of heartbreak. "We're big believers in the healing power of creativity so the songs that were written shortly after we lost Della are darker than the ballads we wrote for the first album."

"How have you been coping with her death? We've heard you've just been released from rehab.."

Joshua cuts Cameron off before he can say any more. "I'd like to stay focused on the new album and not delve into their personal lives."

As Cameron nods, I hold up my hand. "I'll answer the question. I'm sure it's one I'll get a lot so let's just put it out there. I don't have anything to hide. I'm a recovering alcoholic. Della helped me get sober and I'd been sober for quite some time. When I lost her, I fell off the wagon pretty hard.   I struggled with an enormous amount of depression and when it became obvious that I couldn't handle things on my own, I admitted myself into a month long intensive therapy rehab program in

California. I've been sober for almost two months."

Cameron gives me a thumbs up and I continue. "The guys in this room are my family and when I looked at the hard truth, I realized I wasn't just hurting myself. They were afraid they'd lose me too and when one of them laid the truth out in front of me, I realized I needed help. I'm stronger than I've ever been. I think we all are. We're ready to release this new album and head back out on the road. I'm happy and healthy and I've had more therapy than any person should ever have in a lifetime."

They all laugh and I join in when I realize how far we've all come. Even Joshua smiles and I know that I've said all I need to say. The subject is closed, as it should be. The press will make up whatever stories they feel they need to. People will make assumptions about all of us and no matter what we say, stories will never be completely true. I have to learn to let it go. The opinions that matter are the ones in this room and the one of the beautiful woman sitting at home waiting for me.

"The album, entitled Adella, comes out on Valentine's Day. I think it's the best work you've ever done. We'd love to play the title track off the album now. Will you stick around for a few more questions after the song?"

Joshua agrees and I excuse myself. I need a few minutes and a few more deep breaths. My heart swells when Cameron announces the name of the album. When I returned from rehab, I had my first chance to see the cover. It knocked the wind out of me. It was a blurred out picture from our wedding and said nothing but Adella. I'd cried like a baby that night when I was alone. The gesture was more meaningful than anything in my entire life.

I'd found out later that night that Max had written the ballad about Dell and the love we'd shared during our short time as husband and wife. It was dark and powerful and gave me the chills every time I heard it. Recording it was difficult but the tribute to her was beautiful. Max had insisted that the album not only be dedicated to her, but be titled Adella, after the woman that brought us all together. It was that moment that I decided that Max loving her was also a gift to me. Had he not loved her the way he did, we wouldn't be releasing the most amazing work we've ever done. We wouldn't be releasing it on Valentine's Day and it would've been named something that held little meaning for me.

Max's love for Della also made me realize that he had so much to offer someone. I wanted him to find what I had with her. The decision to fire Rachel was a no brainer. Even in my darkest days, with a brain slurred by alcohol, I could see how he looked at her. In those days, I didn't care if anyone was happy. For me, life had stopped. As I worked through that with her, I realized Rachel was exactly who Max needed. She's strong and dedicated, she's calm and healing and she's absolutely beautiful. He's had sessions with her that exposed his past and she helped him face it with the zest for life that Max always has. I won't ever force the subject, but if she happened to be in the same place that we were at some random time, I won't be surprised when he finds all of us leaving him alone with her. He's so afraid of his past catching up with his future, but we'll all be there when he pulls his head out of his ass and realizes he's worth more than the bullshit that used to define him.

When I hear the song coming to an end, I take a deep breath and find myself smiling. I'm looking forward to the day we perform it live. I can't wait to feel the energy of the crowd, the intensity of Damien's voice and the love that radiates from all of us standing together as we remember the woman that changed everything.

"You alright?" Damien pokes his head out of the sound booth and I smile.

"I'm good." I nod to reassure him. And I am. I really am.

He holds the door for me as I join the men that have made the last few months less painful, less dark and less hopeless.

If this plane doesn't land in the next few minutes, I'm going to lose my mind. The record snowfall in most of the country has delayed or cancelled flights all over. Laney's flight has been delayed twice but I'm too excited to leave the airport. I've gotten to know my new bodyguard a little too well. The bright side is that I've met some fans that are stranded here in New York for the time being. I've taken selfies with almost all of them. I've heard some incredible stories about how our music has influenced them and have a new found faith in the human spirit.

I know I've driven Laney crazy over the past week. On average, I think we've talked eight times a day. I'd call her more often but she needs to sleep at some point and I'd hate to come across too strong. Shit. Who am I kidding? The woman should be running for the hills. Yet, she answers every call with a smile on her face and a promise to see me soon.

The words 'I love you' have been on the tip of my tongue for weeks. She deserves to know how I'm feeling. I've been terrified to say them out loud. But, earlier this week, I overheard a conversation between Damien and a very sick Mia. She came down with the flu right after we left and quarantined herself in their bedroom. Damien's been worried about her and watching him pour his heart out makes me realize that I want exactly what they have. I want the phone call to check on me when I'm sick. I want to worry about someone because they're my priority. Sometime during this week away from Lane, I realized I already have that. And I'm the luckiest son of a bitch on the planet. I had it with Della and I have it again with Laney.

I get a second 'once upon a time' and I'm not going to waste a single second of it. I'm going to live in the now and tell her how I feel every chance I get.

As passengers start filing into baggage claim, I see her right away. Her hair is pulled into two short braids and she's wearing yoga pants and a sweatshirt. I don't know when yoga pants became so sexy but she can wear the shit out of them. When she sees me, her grin spreads across her whole face. I jog toward her and pull her into my arms, swinging her around as I hug her tighter than I ever have.

The public display of affection gets the attention of more people than I imagined it would. Honestly, I don't give a shit. She hasn't been in my arms for a week and she isn't leaving them for even a second. People are pulling out cell phones and snapping pictures or video. The moment is anything but private. Still, Laney hugs me and smiles as I whisper how much I've missed her. In one second, we've taken our relationship from something we're taking slow to a public announcement that there's a new woman in my life.

Joe is with her and tries to shield us from unwanted attention.

He's turned into my new favorite guard and I plan on making sure he's with Laney every second I can't be. He pushes through the crowd that's gathered and gets us into the waiting limo. He stands outside the limo, preventing anyone from getting too close as my new bodyguard heads inside to get their luggage. It gives me the opportunity to bury my tongue in her mouth and taste the woman I've fallen head over heels for.

"I know all of this seems fast," I say in between kisses. "You came into my life like a hurricane and fucked shit up." I laugh when she slaps me in the chest. Even her pout is sexy.

I have a lot to say to her and I need her to hear me. "I planned on spending the rest of my life drowning in depression and whiskey. I wanted to give up on everything. You wouldn't let me. You were a pain in my ass when I first met you and you challenged everything I ever said. You were my little guard dog when Della first died and wouldn't let anyone get close enough to hurt me anymore. You sat on the floor and pulled shards of glass out of my leg in the middle of the night when I was too far gone to help myself. Then the next morning, you called me on all my bullshit and threatened to kick my ass. Like I said, my little hurricane."

"Somebody needed to call you on your bullshit. You were disappearing and I cared too much to watch it happen." She rests her head on my shoulder and sighs. "I think I could have taken you too. You didn't have much fight left in you."

"You made me fight for me. I realized how much I cared the night you licked my neck in front of Oksana. You were marking your territory and instead of making me nervous, it made my heart swell with pride." I take a deep breath. Here goes nothing. "The night I came to your apartment for the first time, I wanted to tell you that I was falling in love with you. I was so scared to admit it. I felt like I was cheating on Della by having feelings for you. I made you promise you understood we could never be more than friends and the next morning, I couldn't get out of there fast enough because I knew it was too late. I already loved you."

I look at her and my heart races. Her eyes are filled with tears but the smile on her face tells me they're tears of joy. I smile at her as I wipe the first drops from her cheeks. The woman owns me. She has no idea I'm in this deep. When I love, I love completely.

There will never be anyone in the world that will love her more completely and more fiercely than I will. I'm all in. It's time she knows that.

I take her cheeks in my hands and look her right in the eyes. "I love you Hurricane Adelaine. I'm so in love with you that it scares me that I'll wake up one day and this won't be real."

Her lips meet mine and without words, she tells me everything I need to know. She feels exactly the same way. Our kisses are electric and when we lose ourselves in each other, it's like coming home. I never thought I could feel this way about another person again. It's the scariest thing in the world but if love isn't worth the risk, then nothing is.

"I love you too, Griffin Miles. I don't remember a day before you and I can't imagine a day without you."

I'd lay my life down for this woman and now that I've said it, I plan on spending the rest of my days proving it.

Chapter 23

He loves me. Holy shit. He's being so romantic and his words are so beautiful. I've waited my whole life to hear those words from someone as amazing as he is. As his dark eyes stare at me, love is written all over his face. I have the strangest reaction. I laugh. And when I try to stop, I laugh even harder. He doesn't even look surprised.

"You love me." I cover my mouth to try to stop the giggles. Hello bipolar, my name is Laney.

He kisses the tip of my nose. "I love you." His smile melts my heart.

Joe climbs into the back of the limo as Harley's new bodyguard throws my bags in the trunk. He's become a constant companion in the last week and although it was a pain in the ass at first, he's grown on me. We've been able to joke with each other when Harley calls for the third time during the morning. We've eaten dinner together and tried to solve the problems of the world. I feel safe when he's around and I trust him completely. I wonder if this is how Della felt with Lex. I pray it isn't. Joe knows more about Lex and Oksana than he's willing to tell me. The constant whispering with Joshua confirms it. I don't ask. I'm just happy he's protecting me. And I'm praying he isn't staying anywhere near my hotel room. I plan on spending some time getting loud with this gorgeous man who loves me.

The driver starts the car and I know our alone time is over. I lean into him and purr in his ear. "Prove it."

He sighs and closes his eyes. I 'accidently' brush my fingers over the bulge in his jeans and smile to myself when I see his body's reaction. He shifts in the seat and grabs my hand in his. He squeezes it and gives me a warning with just a look. This is going to be fun.

The drive into Manhattan won't take long. I rub my leg against Harley's. When he sits up a little straighter, I continue the game. I unbuckle my seatbelt and lean forward to grab a bottle of water from the bar. My ass is eye level in front of him and I hear him groan. Just one wiggle before I sit down. My inner slut giggles. I take off my jacket, and stretch. My t-shirt rises about an inch.

I know my belly ring is a turn on for him so I make sure it shows.

He gets restless. When he can't sit still, I know I've got him. He stares out the window and takes some deep breaths. The two body guards are too lost in conversation to pay any attention to me. I fold my jacket in my lap, making sure to cover his too. My hand dips underneath and I rub against his erection. His eyes snap to mine and I bite my lip.

"Lane." It's just a whisper but it holds a warning that I'm going to ignore.

I arch my back, stretching again. "I'm so stiff from the flight. So stiff."

He leans into me and whispers, his voice laced with passion. "Not as stiff as I am."

It sends a bolt of electricity straight between my thighs. I'm going to pay for this later. I can't wait. I smile at him and he returns it. His grin is evil and laced with the promise of retaliation. He grabs my hand and his thumb rubs circles against my palm. I close my eyes and imagine his thumb rubbing against my clit in exactly the same way. My core throbs. I rest my head against the seat and picture him between my legs, licking me the way he does, his magic tongue demanding I come. My breathing gets shallow and I feel Harley let go of my hand and put his arm around me instead.

As the car stops in front of the hotel, Joe tells us he's going to check our surroundings. "Hold tight. We'll get you out of here in a few minutes."

Harley pulls me into a hug. When the door slams, he's ripping his jeans open. "I'm so fucking hard, I can't wait another second. I need to come."

As he reaches for me, I stop him. We only have a few minutes and I want it to be all about him. I drop to my knees in front of him, taking his erection into my mouth. He doesn't say a word as I start to work him. His hands tangle in my hair, guiding me up and down his shaft as he fucks my mouth. I let him set the pace and take every inch he gives me. I want to make him shatter.

"We have to stop." His whole body shakes as he pulls me away. "Fuck, Laney. We have to stop. I'm so close. This isn't fair to you. I need to make you feel good."

The crowd has gathered outside the hotel as rumors of the band's arrival spread. It may be chaos outside but the tinted windows shield us from the outside world. His eyes are shut and he struggles to get his breathing under control.

I stop him from zipping his jeans. I want him to come. I want to step out of this limo and know what I just did to him. There's no way I'm letting him stop. "I want to finish."

I don't wait for him to say anything. His skin is burning hot as I take him into my mouth again. His breath catches and I moan. As he lifts his hips to meet my mouth, I know he's close. His hands shake and his breathing picks up. His growl is primal as he empties himself into my throat. His whole body convulses and I smile.

He grabs my cheeks and pulls me to him. His lips are hungry and he struggles to control his breathing. "I love you, Lane." His smile lights up his face. "You're amazing."

I love this man more than I've ever loved anyone.

I sit in the audience of one of the nation's top morning talk shows. I'm giddy with excitement knowing Harley and the rest of the guys will be out performing in just a few minutes. I'm so damn proud of all of them. What a year!

As the guys are announced, the girls go crazy. The screams fill the audience and even those outside hold up signs and cheer. 'Marry me, Harley.' 'Mad for Max.' I love it. I'm smiling like a crazy person and cheering right along with them. They're in rare form this morning.

Damien's hair is sticking straight up and he's doing his voice impressions. Chance is flirting with the woman behind the camera. Max is being Max, sitting quietly, just taking everything in.

Harley is the most transformed. His smile is no longer forced, he's relaxed and he's ready to play their tribute song to Della. It's so beautiful and I can't wait to hear it live.

"Welcome. I would say you have some fans in the audience." The host laughs and tries to calm everyone down. "I'm pretty sure these guys no longer need an introduction."

The crowd screams again. When I was younger, I saw 'N Sync on the plaza. I remember thinking that it was so loud and I couldn't believe they could hear the music behind them. I remember holding up a sign for Justin, my hair in pig-tails, braces. I was ridiculous. And today, I get to sit here and smile as the men I love take the stage. I get to see all the young girls, hair in pig tails, going crazy for the eye candy on set. I should have brought a sign. I make a mental note to make the shiniest sign for the next concert. I can't help but laugh at myself.

"In a little bit, they'll be performing their brand new title track, Adella. But first, we need to ask what's on everyone's mind. When is the big wedding?"

Damien laughs and one woman yells 'I love you D'Rey'. "I love you too." Screams. "Mia and I are keeping the date a secret. We're going to do our best to keep it as private as possible."

"Speaking of privacy, Twitter went crazy last night with news on another one of you. In fact, trending in the US last night, was a little story about a mystery woman and Harley."

Harley's jaw drops. "We were trending?" His belly laugh makes me giggle.

Max looks so guilty and Harley notices it too. When he raises his eyebrows at Max, he puts up his hands in surrender. "Fine. I may have leaked a video of you at the airport and I may have posted it on our website."

"Trending later will be the story of how Harley kicks Max's ass, part two." Chance high fives Damien. I love Chance's wit.

"So, tell us, who is this mystery woman?"

Harley shakes his head. That's my guy. "It's been a long year for me. I've been blessed with an incredible relationship in the face of all the darkness. I'm going to enjoy this one in private a little longer."

"Fair enough." The host shakes their hands. "You guys ready for the television debut of Liquid Regret's newest title track?"

I scream right along with the crowd. Being a part of Harley's life is going to have its ups and downs but when times get hard, I will remember the way he looks right now. His smile lights up the entire room and I know his heart beats for me.

"One, two, one, two, three, four." Max taps out the beat on his drum-sticks before Harley and Chance begin their guitar duel through the most haunting song I've ever heard. Damien's voice joins in. It's raspy and sexy as hell. The lights flash, the music echoes. I'm completely mesmerized as I watch Harley get lost in the song. His eyes close and his face transforms with the most beautiful expression I've ever seen.

"Thank you, Della." I whisper. "Thank you for making him the man he is."

Chapter 24

The breeze blows through the trees as I kneel in the place that changed everything. The ground is softer now, the dirt has turned to grass and it doesn't feel as cold as it once did. I run my hand over the granite and take a deep breath.

"A whole year." I get choked up as I look at the date on her headstone. "Things have changed so much, kiddo. I wish you could be here to see it. Our first album went platinum. Can you believe it? I know you're watching us because I am playing better than I ever have."

The wind picks up. "Hi, baby. We all miss you so much. You'd be so proud of Max. He's crazy about Rachel. He told me last night that he thinks you sent her to him. I guess I believe that too. She came to us when you left us. That can't be a coincidence. And Damien and Mia are talking about trying to have a baby as soon as they get married. That blows my mind."

"Lex is dead. He was stabbed before he even made it to trial. I don't know how it happened but I have my suspicions. If I'm right, it was the most amazing gift anyone could have given me. Maybe that makes me crazy, but I can't be sorry about that."

"Joshua smiled once this year. You would have been proud of him." I laugh through my tears. "Chance is still Chance. But he saved me. I'll never be able to repay him for that. He'd had enough and when I saw how angry he'd gotten, I couldn't keep doing this to them. I'm sorry I started drinking again. I just didn't know how I was going to be able to face the rest of my life without you. How do you spend the first half of it with someone you love so much and then they're just gone? I didn't breathe for months."

"I could feel you with me every single day in rehab. Thank you for not giving up on me. Thank you for loving me as much as you did. I don't know what I ever did to deserve you, Dell. I don't know what I did to deserve two amazing women. I don't take any day for granted now. When the day comes that I finally get to see you again, I want you to give me one of those gorgeous smiles and tell me I did things right the second time around."

I look back at my family standing a few yards behind me. Their encouragement has gotten me through the worst days of my life. "Laney's great. I love her so much and I can't believe she picked me. I can't believe that you knew long before I did. You were right, Dell. She's the person I want to be with for the rest of my life. Part of the reason I love her so much is because she loved you. She takes one day at a time with me. She helped me find an amazing new house and the first thing she did was hang a picture of you in the living room. The only other person I know that would've done something like that is you. Thank you for teaching me how to love."

I turn and wave everyone over to me. "We wanted to come out and play our new song for you. Max wrote it for you and it's the best piece of music we've ever done. It's been number one for seven weeks in a row now."

"Not surprising since it was inspired by Della." Chance sits down with his guitar in his lap.

Max smiles as we begin to play. He drums the rhythm onto the grass while we all play the song that means more than anything. The wind picks up and we all look up to the sky as the sun breaks through the clouds. Even Joshua sheds a tear as the song comes to an end. It's been a terrible, beautiful journey that I wouldn't trade for anything.

We spend the next hour laughing and telling stories. It's like Della is with us and it's exactly what we all needed. Laney sits on my lap and Rachel sits a little closer to Max. I smile at her and she shrugs her shoulders. I'm going to enjoy having a front row seat as they fall in love.

I'm wide awake at two in the morning. The new house is so quiet at night and it's hard to sleep. Laney's quiet snores comfort me. I pull her into me and wrap my body around her like I do every night. She'll wake up soon enough. Her voice full of sleep, she'll cuss me out for making her so warm. I'll promise to stop touching her and until her snores start again, I'll keep the promise. Once I know she's asleep, I'll pull her into my warm body again. And we'll repeat the argument again about an hour later. I've never been big on cuddling but Laney is a game changer.

She sighs and I brace myself for the first round of arguing. Instead, she surprises me and rolls on top of me. Her kiss is gentle as her fingers caress my cheeks. I try to enjoy the moment but I can feel myself hardening underneath her. I'm not sure there has been a kiss in the last few months that didn't lead to me making her come. I can't get enough of her. I fit inside her perfectly and her body glides over mine like it was made for me.

She wiggles against me and I can feel her heat against my stomach. She scoots back and runs my cock through her wetness. It's hot and slick and I want to slip inside her. I try to slow my breathing and take my time. We make love every morning and we fuck every night. I'm not sure which one she'll want right now but whatever it is, I'm going to enjoy feeling her soak my cock.

"I want to taste you." My voice cracks like I'm going through puberty. I'm so horny. I just need a taste.

She crawls up my chest and straddles my face. This is my favorite position. The view is amazing and feeling her orgasm shoot through her body before it hits my lips is beyond anything I've ever experienced. I reach around and stroke myself as she begins to move. My tongue flicks over her clit as fast as I can move it. She pulls the piercing in her nipple and throws her head back. Seeing her like this is so beautiful. She's so sensual and lets herself enjoy everything in the bedroom with no reservation.

"I'm close." Her breath comes out in spurts. Her thighs start to shake. I stroke myself even harder as she grinds herself against me. She comes so hard that she has to hold on to the headboard. My face is soaked and I'm in heaven.

"I need to fuck you." She moves my hand and slams down onto my cock. I'm buried to the hilt and I almost come on the first stroke. I try to slow her down but she's too far gone. She circles her hips over and over again. I feel her walls start gripping me harder and I roar her name as she spasms around me. I can't control myself. I sit up and hold her tightly against me and fuck her with everything I have.

"You feel so fucking good." My erection slides in and out so easily. She's soaked and I'm about to come.

She leans away from me and arches her back. With her perfect tits in my face, I'm a goner. I pump two more times and I explode into her, coming harder than I ever have in my life. I keep going until I can't move anymore.

She falls on top of me on the bed and we stare into each other's eyes as we catch our breath. Her blue eyes sparkle with desire. I want to hold her like this all night.

When she eases off of me, I miss her instantly. She stands up and heads for the bedroom door.

"Where are you going?" I yawn as she turns around.

"I'm getting you an energy drink." She giggles.

I look at the clock. It's the middle of the night. "What the hell for?"

"I plan on fucking all night. With our without you, Griff." That evil grin makes my cock stir.

As she walks out of the room, I yell after her. "Hey, Lane? Better get yourself one too. It's going to be a long night."

Chapter 25

The darkness closes in on me. It's happening again. I can feel them coming for me. I try to scream but I can't open my eyes. I feel her hand on me and I want to throw up.

"Shhh, Cal. It's ok, baby. It's just me." I can smell her perfume and I can't breathe.

"Stop." My voice is so weak. Shit. I fight the darkness. That's it. Keep breathing. I just need one minute of clarity. I can take him this time.

My hands shake when I hear his belt. The smell of liquor and cigarettes is overwhelming. Fight,

Callum. Wake up! I'm screaming at myself. My eyes flicker. I'm wading through the fog. Rage burns my lungs. I try to hold as still as I can.

"I thought you said you gave him something." The voice is my nightmare. I will kill him if I ever get out of here. That's a promise.

"I did." I can hear her fumbling around in the darkness. "Should I give him something else?"

"Nah. Just hold him still." The zipper.

Not this time. I slam the back of my head into his face. As he falls to the ground, she screams.

"Dad!" My yell echoes through the pool house. They're right outside. Why can't they hear me?

She's panicking and I won't give her the chance to hurt me again. I turn to her and shove as hard as I can. She stumbles but regains her footing.

"Callum?" I can hear my uncle's footsteps. Thank you, God.

"Kent." The room is spinning. I can't get back up. I feel the needle in my arm.

Bright light shocks my eyes as the door is pulled open. Before I give in to sleep, I hear my uncle yelling. My step-mom is screaming back and it's chaos. I can't turn the noise off. I heave and empty the contents of my stomach all over my football jersey.

"What the fuck is going on?"

I reach out and touch my uncle's foot. "Thank you."

Darkness.

Epilogue

"My name is Harley and I'm an alcoholic. It's been exactly one year since my last drink."

The AA meeting tonight is a special one. My support system is all here. My sponsor, Julie, my band, my Lane. And Della. She's never far from me. I smile at all of them as they clap.

Julie comes up to the stage with my new chip. One year sober. I will keep this thing with me every day. Just as she gets ready to speak, Max stands up.

"I'm sorry to interrupt. I was hoping it would be ok if I give him his chip." Julie and I are both confused but knowing Max, he'll will do something much more meaningful.

As he stops next to me, the rest of my band stands up. A feeling of peace blankets me and for a minute, I wonder if I'm going to pass out. I don't know what's happening but Max has tears in his eyes and a chip in his hand.

I look at Julie. She's holding a shiny gold coin in her hand. I look back at Max and the one he's holding is tarnished. My breath catches and I hold on to the podium to center myself.

"Is that?" I can't finish my sentence.

Max nods his head. "There was no way I was letting you bury this with Dell. She believed in you and made me promise her I'd keep you sober. Seeing you put it into the casket was like watching you give up. I knew it would be a long road to get back to this minute but I wasn't willing to let you bury your past when we buried her."

He hands me the chip that I'd kept in my pocket every day before Della died. I run my fingers over it and feel the familiar ridges, the comforting words. "Unity, Service, Recovery." I say to myself. "To Thine Own Self Be True."

I hug Max so hard he can't breathe. "I love you, Cal." I give him a pat on the back and let go.

He laughs and takes a deep breath. "I love you too, brother. We all vow to have your back every day. We'll all stand with you when things get hard and you want a drink and we'll celebrate with you when you don't take one."

As the meeting lets out, I say goodbye to everyone. My heart is full and my life feels complete. I watch the guys as they get in their cars to head their separate ways. Mia hugs Laney goodbye and heads out with Rachel. She's become a part of our family and watching Max forgive his past is worth all the sacrifices we made when we fired her as our grief counselor.

Oksana's trial is set to begin in Southern California next month. I went to see her last week. I stood at the door and couldn't go in. I want to understand why she did what she did. It may not make sense to me but I need to hear it anyway. I need to figure out a way to let go of all my hatred and find a way that forgiveness can take center stage. I will never forget and forgiving will be next to impossible. But living with anger and hate is not the way I want to start the rest of my life. That night, I didn't sleep at all. I regretted not going in but I just wasn't ready. I'll sit in the front row of that courtroom every day while the trial is going on. It'll be the second hardest thing I've ever done in my life.

The autopsy report says Lex was stabbed a total of thirty-two times. It's not a coincidence. I don't say anything because words aren't necessary. I have my theory on who and how but I won't ever ask. We don't talk about it. I just know that revenge is sweet. It wasn't a lesson I wanted to learn but neither was the one on loss and grief.

I reach into my pocket for the hundredth time today. I've been carrying a ring around for the last three days. I don't want to waste any more time and making Laney my wife will make me incredibly happy. I keep trying to find the perfect time to ask her. Damien had such a romantic proposal planned but Laney's simple. She'd rather have me propose first thing in the morning, when our hair is a mess and we're barefoot in the kitchen making coffee. I'll get down on one knee and it won't matter what I say. What will matter is seeing my ring on her finger and knowing my name will be her's one day.

My life was turned completely upside down the day Della died. I stopped breathing that day. I buried myself in liquor and fear and hopelessness. I spent every minute of the day trying to forget or trying to come up with a plan to leave my life behind. Laney stormed into my heartbreak guns blazing. The day I really looked into her eyes, was the day I started breathing again. My heart started beating. It isn't the same as it was. It's stronger. I'm stronger.

I've been to hell and back and I took the guys right along with me. We fought demons and I found my angel. Della will always be a part of our lives. I feel her in the sunshine on my face and the rain and the cold. I feel her in the gentle breeze that blows. I feel her surrounding me with love every time I take a breath. I see her in Laney's eyes and in Max's smile. I no longer need Liquid Courage to face the darkness. I've decided to let love heal my soul.

The End

Stay tuned at the end of this book for a sneak peek at The Fight, Book 1 of The Fight Series by t. h. snyder.

The Liquid Regret Series

Liquid Regret
Damien -2014

Liquid Courage
Harley - 2014

Liquid Assets

Max – Spine 2015

Liquid Redemption

Chance – Summer 2015

Liquid Rein

Joshua - Fall 2015

MJ Carnal with Lance Jones (Harley)

USA TODAY Bestselling Author, MJ Carnal, lives in South Carolina with her husband, daughter, two dogs and four fish. If she isn't writing, she can be found playing with her daughter, watching The Walking Dead with her husband, cheering on the South Carolina Gamecocks, or obsessing over all things Dr. Spencer Reid from Criminal Minds. She loves to hear from readers and writers. She can be reached at mjcarnalauthor@aol.com, on Facebook at www.facebook.com/mjcarnalauthor or on twitter @mjcarnalauthor.

LANCE JONES AS GRIFFIN "HARLEY" MILES

Thank you! Thank you!

To all my readers. Yeah, you. For all of you that pimp my page and share my sales. For you who spend your money to allow me to keep doing what I'm passionate about. For those of you who fall in love with my men or visit me at signings or email me when you're done with a book. For all the "likes" on contests and pictures and for mentioning me on blogs. For leaving reviews on Amazon or Barnes and Noble. For nominating me for everything under the sun. See a trend here? I do. You rock my world. You make me laugh and smile. You allow me to be who I want to be.

Thank you to my family, who have stood by me on this writing journey. My mom, who let me crash upstairs and lock myself away when I had a deadline. And my awesome baby girl, who loves to read and write. I hope that always continues. Rick, Dad, Chris. I love you guys.

LANCE JONES! Thank you for being the absolute perfect Harley. The minute we met in Charleston, I knew you were exactly who I wanted for this series. You have been an incredible support through this whole thing. I've loved the time we've spent together and I can't wait to have you with me at signings. Thanks for letting me torture you through book one so you could have your happily ever after. To learn more about Lance, visit www.facebook.com/LanceJonesTattooFitnessModel

Josh McCann. You make me laugh every single day. Thanks for paving the road for Liquid Regret and being the best damn lead singer any fictional band could ask for. You are the perfect Damien Reynolds and I've loved watching you take the world by storm. Big things are coming your way and I'm excited I have a front row seat. To learn more about Joshua Mcann: www.facebook.com/JoshuaSeanMccannofficial

Michael Meadows! You shot the most amazing cover picture and I'm so blessed I found you. It was the perfect picture of "Harley". You captured exactly what I wanted and made me feel so much the first time I saw it. I am honored to have worked with you on this cover and I'm looking forward to lots more together. For more information on Michael Meadows: www.facebook.com/MichaelMeadowsStudios

Thank you to Marisa at Cover Me, Darling, for making the most amazing book covers on the market. I'm so proud of these covers and I will never be able to thank you enough. You are so talented. Thank you for sharing that talent with me. I'm in awe of the beauty of my covers. To reach Cover Me, Darling: www.facebook.com/covermedarling

To Christine at The Hype PR. You have taken over and absolutely kicked ass. THANK YOU for everything you did to get my name out there. Thank you for your faith in me and my books. My life is better because you are in it. Xoxoxox

To my kick ass beta readers: Janelle, T. A. McKay (Who makes my awesome book trailers) and Ashley. I don't know how I would ever complete a book without you guys. Your encouragement and excitement keeps me going. My favorite minutes of the writing journey are when I hear back from you about how the book made you feel. Thanks for keeping me going, being stubborn, being open to crying, and for loving my men like they're real. More than anything, Thank you for your friendship.

To Kellie Montgomery. I will never use another editor. You keep me on my toes and make yourself available whenever I need you. Thanks for the mad dash to finish this one. I can't wait to share all my other books with you. You are my sunshine. Xoxox.

To all the blogs that share and pimp and believe in me. I would be nothing without you. The job you do is hard and you spend endless time promoting and reading and loving the written word. I cannot thank you enough. You are the entire world to an author. Thank you for giving up hours of your personal life to promote the authors you believe in. Thanks for allowing me to be one of them!

To the authors who mean the world to me. Thank you for creating the worlds I get lost in. Thank you for your friendship and your encouragement. Thank you for the men I love and the woman I aspire to be.

To my friends. You accept me for my crazy brain and dirty mind. You allow me to cry and bitch and laugh. You hold my hand through the hard times and cheer for me during the good days.

To my street teams. I love you hard. I wish I had you with me in person every single day. My life is beautiful because you add sunshine and love.

And last, but certainly not least! t. h. snyder. Thanks for introducing me to Lance. Thanks for sharing him at signings. Thanks for believing in me. AND THANK YOU for sharing the first chapter of your new book with me and my readers. You are a rock star!

The Fight

Fight Serial Series, #1

By t. h. snyder

Published by t. h. snyder

Prologue

October 18, 2004

HANK

Running around the paper plates in the back alleyway, I round the make shift bases. Out of breath and my chest now heaving, I see my best friend Mike bending down for the flattened kick ball.

Should I do it?

Could I make it home before he gets to me?

With adrenaline rushing through my veins, I pick up speed and sprint as fast as I can to the final base.

"Run, Hank, run," my brother Trenton yells from against the brick wall. "He's coming."

Turning my head, I see Mike is gaining on me. With his right arm, he lifts the ball into the air and tosses it toward me.

As the ball comes at me in slow motion, I decide to make a run for it sliding into home plate. With the rough, rocky ground tearing at my side, I wince in pain as my foot lands on the paper plate.

"Safe," Trenton calls, the ball bouncing beside my left leg. "Good going, *Flash*! We won."

Feeling pride for the winning run, I flatten myself onto the ground attempting to catch my breath.

"Boys, let's go," Ma's voice yells from the house. "We're going to be late for Taryn's birthday party...what the hell are you doing Hank? We need to leave and you're lying in the middle of the filthy alley."

"Yeah yeah, Ma we'll be in soon," I reply sitting up off the ground, wiping the gravel from my bruised hands.

"Hank Clarence Jones, get your ass in this house now!" Ma yells, giving me a look like she's about to kick my ass.

Oh shit!

Rolling my eyes, I know she means business by throwing out the full name. Grunting out a moan of frustration, I lean over to pick up the kickball.

"Fine, we'll be right there."

Buzz kill.

"Trenton, grab the plates," I shout to my twin brother as I move to get up.

Mike moves along next to me laughing as the rest of the guys wave and head down the alley.

"What's so funny?" I ask, waving back to our friends.

"I'd much rather wait and watch her pull you into the house by your ear again, now that was funny."

"Shut up, ass. It only happened once and that's because you wouldn't help me bring the bikes into the tool shed."

Shaking his head, he bends over in a fit of laughter.

"What's so funny?" Trenton asks walking into the conversation.

Gritting my teeth, I look to him and blow out a burst of air in frustration.

"Nothing, let's get inside before Ma comes out again."

Following my brother and best friend up the concrete steps, I'm not exactly sure why we even have to go to Taryn's birthday party. Just because our families are close, doesn't mean that I have to spend the rest of my afternoon with her.

Ugh, that girl gets under my skin in more ways than one; I can't quite put my finger on it. She just drives me nuts.

As I walk into the mud room of our house, Ma is standing there tapping me, I feel a hard smack to the base of my neck.

"Get up stairs, clean up and be down here in ten minutes. Trenton that goes for you, too. Michael go home and get changed. We're leaving in fifteen, no later. "

Refusing to turn around, I stomp my feet against the old wooden floors toward the stairs and up into my bedroom.

"Don't give me attitude, Hank. Move it," her stern voice echoes through the walls.

Sitting in the corner of the Morris' back porch, I tear at the hem of my tee-shirt. This party is lame I want to go home. I don't know anyone here really other than my parents, my twin brother and my best friend;

each of them wrapped up in something more entertaining than me.

I look around at the people gathered here today to celebrate Taryn's sweet sixteen birthday, no one paying any mind to me. Trenton is wrapped up in his girlfriend Lisa, while Mike is stuck to Taryn's side like a love sick puppy dog. I don't get it, Lisa is a whore and Taryn is...well she's Taryn. I can't stand either one of them with their prissy attitudes. I mean, I guess they're pretty and all, but I'm not the type of guy to give up my life for a girl. The guys are so stuck on them that we barely get any time to chill just us anymore. It sucks.

A hand falls onto my shoulder and I snap out of my fog. Looking to my left, I see Monica, Taryn's next door neighbor. Ignoring her presence, I turn away and look out into the backyard.

The Morris' house is a lot better than ours. It's on the other side of town where the wealthier middle class families live. Off of the porch is a backyard that actually has a tree and grass, unlike the dirt and concrete sidewalk in ours. I guess that's what you get when your parents have money. Mr. Morris owns a gym downtown and does some other stuff on the side. As for Mrs. Morris, she's a business woman of some sort out in the city. She travels a lot and leaves Taryn home alone, at least that's what Mike has told me. Works for him in more ways than one, I suppose.

"Hank," a soft voice whispers in my ear.

Swatting her away like a fly, I move to stand from the chair, walking to the other side of the back porch. Feeling her presence behind me, I turn toward her freckled face.

"What's up, Monica?"

Resting her hand on my arm, she bats her makeup filled lashes in my direction.

"I wanted to say hi to you."

"Good job, you just did," I reply bending down to grab a soda out of the cooler.

"Why do you have to be so mean to me all the time? I don't get it."

"What's to get, Monica, I'm not interested."

"You're not interested in girls at all…or just me."

Snapping my head to face her, I don't even want to give her the satisfaction of a response. Hell no! I'm not interested in her or in anything she's willing to give me.

Leaning against the side of the house, she crosses her arms against her chest. With her slight movement, my eyes catch sight of her tight shirt as she pushes her tits up to the top of it.

Being the sixteen year old that I am, with hormones raging, I begin to feel tightness building in the crotch of my jeans.

Not now…not with her.

My eyes gaze up to her bright baby blues, a smile spreading across her face.

Taking a step toward me, she rests her index finger against my chest, running it up to my collar bone. A slight breeze picks up causing her sweet smelling vanilla perfume to hit my senses. Closing my eyes for a brief moment, I try to focus on anything but the situation standing mere inches from me. Her smell is so sweet, her body moving closer to mine and my dick growing harder by the minute.

Focus Hank...not her.

Her body touches mine as my eyes open. Red hair whips into my face as the breeze picks up again, her sweet vanilla scent now wafting directly below my nose. Opening my eyes, I can see that she's moved so much closer to me and she's now biting down on her lip.

"Give me a chance, Hank. I swear you won't regret it," she purrs into my ear.

Good Lord, strike me now. I don't know how much stronger I can be. Letting go of what I don't want from her, I decide to give in knowing I'll be able to walk away with my head held high. At least I'll get a blow job out of the deal.

With my nod of agreement, she grabs my hand and pulls me to follow her. Watching as her hips sway with each step, her ass hugging the material of her tight jeans, she moves us behind the house and down the road. Pulling through the white picket fence, she leads me into the tool shed of her parent's backyard.

Shutting the door behind us, it's practically black inside with only the sunlight casting a streak of light through the crack between two wooden doors.

"Monic…"

"Shhh, no talking," she says before placing her lips against mine.

Without a second to breathe, her tongue is ramming itself into my mouth. Rather than fight the fact that she wants this, I take control of the kiss. Running my hands through her hair, I suck her tongue into my mouth while she begins to unfasten the button of my jeans.

I know where this is leading. Monica has a reputation and I'm not one to say no to a blow job, not when she has me this close, my dick begging for her to suck on it.

She breaks away from the kiss and falls to her knees, digging her small fingers into the opening of my boxers. Leaning back onto the inside wall of the shed, I close my eyes envisioning the same thing taking place, just *not with her.*

Wetness begins to coat my shaft as her tongue starts to twirl up and down.

Reaching forward, I let my hands fall into her hair and guide her head up and down as she sucks me harder into her mouth.

Sounds from outside the shed start to come closer, but I ignore them as the feeling becomes overwhelming. I can feel myself getting ready to blow, it won't be long now.

Suck me harder...faster.

God, this feels so good, if only it wasn't Monica giving me the blow job from heaven. My eyes start to roll into the back of my head as the creaking of the door opening makes a sound and sunlight flashes before my closed lids.

Quickly I open my eyes to see Taryn standing before me, tears in her eyes.

What the...

Pushing Monica away, I pull up my jeans against my now rock hard dick to run out of the shed and after Taryn.

Calling her name as I chase after her, she continues without stopping to pay me any attention.

Making it to her backyard, she's slumped along the steps leading up to the back porch. Sticking her palm out to me, I watch as her breath becomes erratic.

"Don't you dare come any closer to me, Hank Jones," she mutters between sobs.

"Taryn, it's not what…"

"Don't!" she shouts at me. "Monica told me you two were…we'll it's obvious what you two are. I just never imaged you to do it…*not with her.*"

"What are you talking about, her and I are nothing," I reply, anger beginning to rage inside of me that she's so upset over all this.

"What I just saw…that wasn't nothing, Hank," she says flailing her hands in front of her face.

I don't know what to make of all this, she's with Mike…my *best* friend. I can't stand her half the time we're together. Why the hell is she freaking out over nothing and why am I feeling so god damn defensive?

"Come on, Taryn, you've done it with Mike a hundred times."

"Whhhhat? I've never done anything with Mike; he's like a brother to me. I'd never do anything with anyone but…."

Standing to walk away from me she walks up onto the porch, slamming the back door shut.

I'm so baffled, so lost, that my world is spinning right here in front of me.

What just happened and why are Taryn and I both so upset because of it? Confusion and an aching pain from blue balls sets in as I crash into the stairs, my head falling into my hands.

Stay tuned for more of *the Fight* coming December 1, 2014